Finally My Forever

By:

Brooke St. James

Other titles available from Brooke St. James:

Another Shot:
A Modern-Day Ruth and Boaz Story

When Lightning Strikes

Something of a Storm (All in Good Time #1)
Someone Someday (All in Good Time #2)

Chapter 1

It all began when I was seventeen years old. It was the summer before my senior year when I first met him. It was likely our paths would have never crossed in a city the size of San Antonio, but an odd chain of events led me straight to his door.

Let me back up a little.

I'd gotten into some trouble with my parents, but as you could probably guess, none of it was my fault. My mom and stepdad had to pick me up from the police station one evening, but they waited until the next morning to sit down and lecture me about it. I thought they'd decided to drop it since I explained the night before that I was an innocent bystander, but apparently they had other plans.

I knew I was in for it when my mom flung open the door to my room and stormed in, announcing that she and Mike would like to see me in the dining room. The dining room meant they wanted to sit at the table—not on the couch where we could be comfortable, but at the table where I had to look straight at them and see just how disappointed they were.

It was 9:00 in the morning, and I was still half asleep, but they were both dressed. My mom's hair was perfectly pinned up into a bun, and Mike looked like he'd already been out playing golf.

"You're lucky they're not pressing charges, Carly Michelle," my mom said, staring down at me with her arms crossed indignantly. It was the first thing that came out of her mouth, and I wasn't quite prepared for how angry she was. I thought we were going to sit at the table like civilized adults, but she and Mike had a chair pulled out into the middle of the room, and they instructed me to sit in it while they both stayed standing. I sat there sitting on my hands as they paced in front of me like a couple of detectives interrogating a suspect.

"It wasn't my fault," I said for the tenth time since they picked me up last night. "I didn't know we weren't supposed to be there."

My mom glared at me as if she was scared that I was losing my mind. "What exactly did you think, Carly, when you had to *climb a fence?*" She was extremely agitated. Her eyes were bulging out of her head, and she spit out the words angrily.

"Calm down Rhonda," my stepdad said, playing good cop.

Her mouth formed into a flat line, and she squinted at him while pointing at me. Whatever was about to come out of her mouth was going to be delivered in really dramatic fashion—I could tell from her expression. "I'll calm down, Mike, when Little Miss Trouble With The Law explains why she thought *trespassing and starting a fire on private property* was a good idea!" She started the sentence

5

at a reasonable volume, but was yelling by the time she finished it.

"Mom, you're acting like we started a forest fire," I interjected. "It was a bonfire, and it was in a spot where other bonfires had been lit before. Nothing got burned down. It wasn't that big of a deal. I don't even know why they called the cops."

She coughed out a laugh. "They called the cops, Carly, because you were *trespassing on their property*!" It seemed as if all her sentences were destined to end with her yelling the last few words. Her face was completely red as she stared down at me.

"Calm down, Mom."

"Your mother has every right to be angry, Carly," Mike said in a calm tone. "This isn't the first time you've ended up in the wrong place at the wrong time recently. We're both worried that it's going to become a habit."

"It's Gigi," my mom said, shaking her head and crossing her arms again. "I could see a mile away that girl's not a good influence. I don't think she owns a single shirt that covers her entire stomach."

I felt like rolling my eyes, but I didn't. I just stared up at them with what I hoped was an expressionless face. They stared back at me for several long seconds before my mom stuck her hand out in my direction and looked at my stepdad. "See?" she said, "She's completely unremorseful!"

"I'm just sitting here, Mom. What do you want me to do—bust out crying?"

"It would be better than just sitting here staring at us like you don't even care that you got *arrested* last night, Carly!"

"I do care, Mom, but there's nothing I can really do about it, is there?"

"Oh you're gonna pay. Don't you worry about that."

I looked at my stepdad for some support.

"We were thinking some community service might be appropriate," he said.

I stared at the ceiling and let out a sigh.

"And you're taking a break from your phone and car for about a week too," my mom added.

I glowered at them with my mouth hanging wide open. "That's not fair at all!" I said.

My mom was still shaking her head and staring at me with a stone faced expression like I was some sort of hardened criminal. I decided I needed to change my tactics if I wanted any chance of reasoning with them. I stuck my hands in the air in a gesture of surrender, and began speaking softly as if they were both bombs that were about to explode.

"Okay, let me just explain what happened last night so you can see that none of it was my fault and it wasn't that big of a deal."

I paused and my mom's eyes widened as she waited for me to continue. They both looked angry and disappointed, which made it hard for me to concentrate on my story. I glanced down and took a few seconds to remember the chain of events.

"There were about eight of us hanging out last night at Gigi's, and this guy Brice said he knew of a place we could go to light a bonfire. He said he went there all the time."

I glanced at my mom. She was still wearing a mask of anger, but I tried not to let it effect me. She didn't look like she was going to budge, but I knew I didn't deserve a punishment this severe, so I had to start talking my way out of it. I sighed, trying to gather my thoughts.

"Gigi's parents gave us permission. Her mom even went to the store and bought us stuff to make smores before we left."

I paused and she scoffed. "So you're trying to convince us you had *permission* to go break the law."

"I'm saying none of us knew we were doing anything wrong until the cops came. It wasn't a big deal. We were just out in the woods hanging out."

She squinted at me. "Didn't it strike you as odd that you had to climb a fence to get in there, Carly?"

"We didn't climb a fence, Mom. There was a gate with a chain, but it opened big enough for us to walk through easily. Brice said we couldn't drive the cars through it, but he didn't say anything about us not being allowed back there on foot. He said he knew the owners."

"Just because he knows the owners, doesn't mean he had permission, obviously. You're lucky nobody's pressing charges, young lady," she repeated.

"She's lucky they didn't burn anything down," my stepdad added.

"Brice acted like it was fine for us to be out there," I said shrugging.

They both stared at me.

"You really should have known better," Mike said. "Especially with the chain on the gate."

My mom sunk her face into her hand with a dramatic sigh. "People are going to find out about this. Even though charges weren't pressed, they're gonna find out you guys were in trouble." She looked into my eyes with sincere disappointment. "You know how important it is to keep a good name, Carly. Is this what you want people to think about when they hear the name Carly Howard—someone who's in trouble with the law?"

"No, Mom, but I didn't—"

"You got arrested, Carly. You rode in the back of a patrol car to the police station. It doesn't matter if it was your fault or not. You put yourself in a compromised position, and now you have to suffer the consequences."

I couldn't believe they were still going to punish me. I let out a defeated sigh and let my shoulders slump. "What do you guys expect me to do for community service?" I said, hoping to get it over with.

"I'm bringing you over there in a few minutes," Mike said.

I regarded them with a dumbfounded expression. "Today?"

Mike looked at his watch. "I told Jesse I'd have you over there before 10. That gives you fifteen minutes or so to get ready."

I couldn't believe what I was hearing. I gawked at them. "Over where? Who's Jesse?"

"Mr. Bennett to you," Mike said. "Jesse Bennett is one of my clients at work. He's a general contractor."

"What's that got to do with me?" I asked.

"He does a lot of work with people with disabilities," Mike explained. "His company built a house in Stone Oak over by where his family lives." He shook his head as if he didn't quite know the whole story. "It's got something to do with their charity work. I think it's a gathering place for people with disabilities. Anyway, they're done with construction and they're having a weekend work party to do things like clean and paint—things to get the house ready for opening. He had us make some t-shirts for all the volunteers."

This did *not* sound like something I could participate in. I shook my head slightly. "I don't think I can do that," I said.

"I don't think you have a choice," my mom said.

I looked at Mike with a pleading expression, begging him to see the flaws in this idea. "I'd just be in their way," I said. "I don't know anything about construction."

"All these people are volunteers," he said.

I shifted my attention to my mom and gave her my best *please help me* face. "I don't know any of these people," I said. "Please don't make me do this."

"I think you need it," she said. "Mike says they're a good family, and I think it's just what you need right now."

"What's that supposed to mean?" I asked.

"It means it'll do you some good to get out of your little high school box and do what you can to help someone else."

She was implying that I was selfish, and I wanted to defend myself, but I knew it would just lead to more arguing.

"They're a good family," Mike said.

"It doesn't change the fact that I don't know anybody there and I'm gonna be totally out of place. I'll just be in their way."

They stared at me with matching unsympathetic expressions. Mike looked at his watch again. "You better get ready," he said. "We'll need to leave in about ten minutes."

I didn't argue. I knew it was no use.

Fifteen minutes later, Mike and I were sitting in the front seat of his truck on the way to Jesse Bennett's house in Stone Oak. I was eating a granola

11

bar when he said, "Your mom was right about keeping a good name, you know. I'll be talking to Jesse, and I expect him to tell me you did a good job today."

I felt blood rise to my cheeks at his words. I was embarrassed, which made me feel angry. I wanted to defend myself, but I held my tongue.

"You hear me, Carly?" he asked, glancing at me.

I wanted to scream, cry, and hit something, but all I said was, "Yes sir."

"Good," he said. "Your mother and I both want what's best for you. We don't want to see you go down the wrong path following the wrong type of people."

There was no use explaining that teenagers all over the world were doing a lot worse things then hanging out with her friends at a bonfire. There was no point in defending myself anymore. I stayed quiet and stared out the window until we arrived at our destination.

"Jesse's wife's name is Claire," Mike said as we stopped in the driveway. "She's expecting you. You'll ride with her to the construction site. Do you want me to walk you up?"

I was already mortified as it was. The last thing I needed was for Mike to follow me up there. He'd probably feel the need to explain that I had been in trouble and give her way too much information. Come to think of it, he'd probably already said all that on the phone.

"No thanks, I got it," I said.

"This is a nice place," he said, peering out of the truck. It was a nice place, but I didn't respond. He put the truck in gear and I opened the door to get out. "She said I could pick you up at six," he said. That made me stop in my tracks. "Six at night?" I asked.

"Well, not six in the morning," he said, sarcastically.

"That's a long time," I said. "I thought I was only staying a few hours."

"There's a lot to do," he said, shaking his head like that was obvious. "I'll see you at six."

I closed the door to the truck without another word. I'm sure my face reflected how enthusiastic I was about the whole thing. I walked up the driveway, past the manicured flowerbeds onto the gorgeous, sprawling porch, and knocked twice on the door. I was expecting a lady to answer, so I was shocked to see what I thought was a guy through the beveled glass windows of the door. It swung open, and it suddenly made sense why this family was charitable to people with disabilities. The guy standing at the door was wearing a smile so big that it looked like his face might break in half. It was a huge, open mouth smile that made it literally impossible for me not to smile back.

"I don't think I know you," he said, still smiling, as he looked me over.

It didn't take a genius to tell he was different, but I didn't know exactly what made him so. He looked like he might have Down Syndrome, but I didn't know anything about different types of disabilities so I couldn't be sure. Just then, the lady I assumed was Mrs. Bennett came up behind him. She looked past me to smile and wave to Mike who was starting to leave. She immediately focused on me with a bright smile. She had long chestnut brown hair that was pulled into a ponytail.

"You must be Carly," she said.

I gave a slight nod. "Yes ma'am."

"Carlyyyy!" the guy said, throwing his arms in the air as if we'd won some sort of championship together.

Something about having someone get so excited when they say your name makes you feel good. My gaze shifted downward with an uncontrollable grin.

Mrs. Bennett put her hand on my shoulder to encourage me to come inside, and I glanced at her as I followed to see that she was smiling warmly. "I'm Claire," she said as I crossed the threshold, "and this is my son Thomas."

Chapter 2

Thomas Bennett put his arm over my shoulders as we made our way into their beautiful home. "We're building a house where all my friends can come play video games, and eat cupcakes, and make crafts... and there's gonna be a ton of books. Do you like to read books?"

Mrs. Bennett had gone ahead of us into the kitchen while Thomas and I lagged behind in the living room. It was a huge, open space, and I could see her at the edge of the counter, gathering some last minute things. I looked back at Thomas, who was anxiously awaiting my answer to his question.

"I do like books," I said.

"What's you're favorite book?" he asked excitedly.

I assumed he had Down Syndrome. I'd seen people with it, but never actually been in a conversation with any of them. The first thing that struck me was how sweet and sincere he seemed. It seemed like he was thrilled beyond words at the prospect of learning about my favorite book.

"I don't read as much as I should, but when I do, I like romance or adventure best, I guess."

"Awww!" Thomas said, slapping a hand to his forehead. "Are you talking about kissing books?"

I stared at him for a second, not really sure how to answer.

15

"Are you talking about the books where they kiss each other?" he repeated, definitely loud enough for his mom to hear.

"Yeah, but I'm a girl," I whispered. "Girls like that sort of thing."

He slapped his hand to his forehead again and shook his head as he laughed. "Girls are so silly!"

"What's your favorite book?" I asked.

His face instantly shifted to one of great sincerity. He was about the same height as me, and we stood eye to eye as he stared at me and said, "Definitely the Bible."

I nodded and smiled. "Oh, yeah, the Bible," I said even though I'd never read it. "I guess I didn't realize that was a choice."

He nodded. "It's a choice," he said. "Do you want to change your favorite book now?"

He was so sweet and sincere that I had to agree. "For sure," I said.

He patted me on the shoulder. "That's good. That's a good choice. It's the best book there is. It's got love in it, you know. It's got everything. It's a whole bunch of books all wrapped up into one." He paused and stared at me intently. "It's the only book in the world like it. You did the right thing changing your choice." He smiled and patted my shoulder again. "I'll bet you just forgot."

"I did," I said.

His mom interrupted us. She was wearing a bright smile and carrying a few bags of supplies along with her oversized purse. "Are you two ready?" she asked.

"Can I help you with any of that?" I asked.

"I think I got it," she said. She extended the arm that was holding the purse. "Thomas, dig in there for my keys, please baby. I'll need you to lock up."

He did as she asked and we made our way to the huge SUV that was parked in the garage. Thomas offered me the front seat, but I told him I was content to ride in the back. The ride to the construction site only took us a few minutes, and Thomas talked the whole time about how cool the house would be and how many great things he and his friends would be able to do there. I assumed by his descriptions that there would be quite a few people helping out today, and I dreaded being the only one there who didn't know anybody.

Mrs. Bennett agreed to let me carry one of the bags inside when we arrived. I was greatly relieved to help since it gave me something to do with my hands. It was heavy and I couldn't believe she had carried that and the others by herself. I looked inside to find two 6-packs of Powerade.

"That's for my baby brother," Thomas said, seeing me glance inside. "He likes the white ones. And Mom likes the white ones because they don't make a mess if you spill."

"I guess everybody likes the white ones," I said. At least I started to say it.

Thomas, catching a glimpse of someone he recognized, cut me off in midsentence. He threw his arms up in the same way he had done for me when we first met. "Valerieeee!" he said.

The girl, who was beautiful and seemed to be in her twenties, made the same gesture with her arms. "Thomasssss!" she yelled. She greeted Mrs. Bennett with a kiss on the cheek. "We're already getting a lot done in there," she said.

"Oh, good," Mrs. Bennett replied, "Thank you for being here."

"I wouldn't miss it for the world."

"Plus, you get that cool t-shirt," Thomas said, proudly. He looked at me with a wide-eyed, serious expression. "You need a shirt too."

"Oh, I'm okay," I said. I was tempted for a split second to add that my dad's company was the one who printed them, but I opted to stay quiet.

Valerie and Mrs. Bennett were talking about all the work that was going on, and I followed them into the house, content with holding my bag of sports drinks and blending into the background.

There were several volunteers visible when we walked in. Two men were laying tile around the fireplace, two were in the kitchen doing something with power tools that required them to wear goggles, and a few more were spread around looking busy. I followed Mrs. Bennett into the kitchen where she commented on how nice the new refrigerator looked and began putting the bottles into it. Thomas and

Valerie disappeared down the hall to go inspect the rest of the house.

"How can I help?" I asked.

"How do you feel about painting?" a man's voice said from behind me. I turned to find a man about my dad's age staring at me with a big smile. He had mostly black hair with some gray on the sides and his eyes were the type that squinted when he smiled.

"Honey, this is Carly," Mrs. Bennett said.

"Mike's daughter!" he said, smiling.

I was his stepdaughter but I didn't correct him. I assumed he must be Mr. Bennett. He stuck out his hand, and kept right on with that squinty-eyed smile. Something about it seemed warm and welcoming. I was glad for it at a time when I felt nervous and out of place. I shook his hand and smiled back.

"I don't know much about painting, "I said, getting back to this question, "but I'd be happy to give it a try."

"It's just a matter of rolling paint on the walls," he said. "We'll come behind you and do the trim. I don't think you can really mess anything up."

He gestured for me to follow him, but then looked over his shoulder at his wife. "Unless you needed her for something," he said. I glanced back to see her smiling and shaking her head.

Mr. Bennett brought me to one of the bedrooms and explained that it would be the arts and crafts room. The walls were being painted a neutral gray so all of their art projects would stand out when hung.

There was another volunteer already working. It was an older lady who Mr. Bennett introduced as Joan. We greeted each other with a wave before Mr. Bennett gave me a three-minute explanation about how to get paint onto the wall without drips and other unwanted things happening.

He didn't question me about my sudden urge to volunteer or imply that he knew anything about me being in trouble. I had been afraid of this sort of confrontation and was happy to avoid it.

For the next little while it was just me and the grey paint. I could hear a radio in the distance along with the sounds of other volunteers talking and banging on things, but mostly, I was alone with my thoughts. Joan asked me a couple of questions at first, but otherwise she didn't say much. She left the room for a few minutes at a time but would always come back and pick up where she left off. We both seemed content to work quietly. I didn't regret being there and helping out with something that seemed to be a good cause, but I still felt like my parents had been a little harsh with the punishment, and I was in a fairly bad mood because of it.

I'd been painting for what must have been over an hour when my neck began to get stiff. I sighed and set the roller down in the pan before stretching my arms upward.

"Joannnn! Carlyyyy!" Thomas said coming into the room right at that moment. His eyes instantly went up to the area where the wall met the ceiling, and his smile changed to a look of concern. He pointed at the area he was staring at. "Are you gonna leave it like that?" he said, his face crumpling into a look of wary confusion.

Joan answered before I could. "Of course we're not, Thomas," she said patiently. "Your dad's gonna come behind us and make it nice and straight with a paint brush."

Thomas sighed and laughed thankfully. He giggled for a few seconds before his face turned serious again. He looked at Joan. "Did you know the Bible is Carly's favorite book?"

"No I didn't!" she said sweetly. She smiled at me and I smiled back a little stiffly. Joan still had her roller in her hand, so she turned her attention back to the wall.

"What's your favorite Bible verse?" Thomas asked with a hand on my shoulder. I could feel the blood rising to my cheeks the second he said it. I'd been to vacation Bible school a couple of times when I was a kid, but otherwise didn't know much about the Bible at all. I knew there was a very famous verse about God so loving the world, and I racked my brain trying to think of it. It took me a second, but I thought I had it right. I smiled as I said, "For God so loved the world that he gave his son—"

"John 3:16!" Thomas said, with his hands in the air.

"That's one of my most favorite verses, isn't it, Ms. Joan?"

"Yep, you love that one, Thomas," she said without turning around.

"It's not my most very favorite one, though," he assured me.

What was there for me to do but ask, "What's your favorite?"

He put his hand back on my shoulder and stared at me with an earnest expression like what he was about to say was a matter of national security. "John 1:29," he said. He cleared his throat in preparation to recite it. "The next day John saw Jesus coming toward him, and said..." Thomas stopped talking and out of nowhere sunk his crumpled face into his hand. He stayed that way for several long seconds.

I glanced around, not knowing what to do.

Joan kept right on working.

I thought Thomas just had his head down, so it startled me when he started making a high-pitched wheezing sound as he breathed out. It took me a second to realize he was crying. He made this sound as he breathed out and then he took a shaky breath in. Once again, a long, wheezing cry came out with his face still covered by his hand.

I glanced at Joan desperate for some help, but she kept right on painting. Thomas let out a few more high-pitched wails before wiping his eyes and trying to compose himself.

He regarded me with a pitiful, tear-soaked face.

"Behold..." he said. Another long, wheezing wail. "John said, Behold! The Lamb of God who takes away the sin of the world." His face was contorted with the effort to hold back tears and his voice was much higher than normal as he said the last part of that verse. He regarded me afterward as if he was gauging how affected I was.

"Is that the whole verse?" I asked. I didn't know what else to say. It seemed really short, and I honestly didn't understand how he was so touched by the simple line he'd just recited.

"Didn't you hear it?" he asked, looking at me as if he was wondering why I wasn't crying.

"Was it just that John saw Jesus and said, Behold, the—"

Thomas cut in, "The Lamb of God who takes away the sins of the..." He lowered his head and breathed out a wheezing cry again. "The world," he concluded after that cry was out of his system.

I glanced at Joan, who still had her back to us being no help whatsoever.

"That's pretty cool," I said.

"It's the most beautiful Bible verse ever," he said. "It's the only thing we need to believe—the one truth we need most of all." He stared at me as if trying to see if I suddenly understood. "God could have been born a big tough guy like with muscles like Micah. He coulda come to earth and punched everybody out who didn't listen to Him." He paused, but continued, "But instead he chose to be born a lamb—" And there it went again. He sank his face into his hand and let out that high-pitched wail.

Joan was still no help, and I looked around wondering what in the world I could do or say.

"Was Micah another person in the Bible?" I asked, in an attempt to distract him. I knew there was a guy in the Bible who was known for his strength, and I assumed after what Thomas said, that he was talking about Micah, which sounded like a Bible name. It was my best bet for trying to distract him from this Lamb verse that made him cry so much.

He had tears streaming down his face, but he looked at me with a big smile. "Micah's in the Bible, but I was talking about my baby brother."

"Oh, you have a baby brother named Micah?" I asked. He smiled and nodded, not even bothering to wipe the tears from his face. I had a towel hanging from my back pocket that Mr. Bennett had given me for drips. I hadn't used it for paint, so I took it out and used it to dry Thomas' cheeks. I sort of expected him to take it from me and do it himself, but he just waited while I patted the tears from his face.

"I wouldn't call Micah a baby," Joan chimed in, finally.

Thomas glanced her way. "He's fifteen months younger than me," he said. "He's nineteen and I'm twenty."

"Yeah but that doesn't make him a baby," she said.

"I'm turning twenty-one soon," he said, trying to strengthen his case. Joan just kept painting and

Thomas looked at me. "Do you know my baby brother?"

I shook my head indicating that I didn't, and without hesitation, he grabbed me by the hand.

Chapter 3

I really didn't feel like being there in the first place, much less being dragged across the house to play meet and greet. I had been so frustrated with my parents about making me come that I'd barely even looked in a mirror beforehand.

"My brother's outside making the patio," Thomas said, pulling me down the hallway. "The stones are really heavy, so I can't help with that. My dad said I have to stay out of his way."

"It sounds like he's busy," I said. "Maybe I can just meet him later."

"No, you can meet him now," he assured me. "We just can't help with the stones. But that's okay because you still have more painting to do. Remember how you missed those spots?"

"Yep, that's why I should probably be getting back in there," I said. I gave him a slight tug in the opposite direction, and his grip tightened.

"I promise you will like my brother," he said. "Every girl likes him."

Before I knew it, we'd walked through the kitchen and Thomas was opening the sliding glass door that led to the backyard. There were three guys on the far side of the patio, and all of them were kneeling as they worked together to try to position a heavy stone.

"Hey Micah, this is my new friend Carly!" Thomas called. All three of them looked our way at Thomas' exclamation. I caught sight of Mr. Bennett first. He was smiling at me and I smiled back as my gaze shifted to the next guy who was about Mr. Bennett's age. I smiled at him for the briefest of seconds before shifting my attention to the third guy—the one who was mostly hidden from my view. The third guy, who I assumed was Micah, stood up to get a better look at me.

I'll never forget the first time I saw him. He had on torn jeans that rode low on his hips and a thin, white, skintight tank top that showed the rows and rows of sculpted muscle underneath. He used his forearm to wipe the sweat off of his brow. He looked like a commercial for... whatever. He could have been selling anything and I'd buy it. He might as well have stood up and wiped his brow in slow motion, that's how picturesque it was. He was comically gorgeous, and I felt myself smiling at the absurdity of the situation.

The other two men went back to the task of shifting the rock as Micah started to walk toward us. I began shaking my head the instant I realized what he was doing. I had no idea what I looked like, but I knew it was bad. There was no way I could let him get close to me. As if shaking my head wasn't enough, I stuck my hand out to stop him. "Don't quit what you're doing," I insisted. "Thomas just wanted to introduce me to his baby brother." I smiled real big and waved as I started to turn with the intention of heading back inside.

"It's okay," Micah said. "I needed to grab some water anyway." He looked at his dad and the other man. "You guys want anything?"

"I'll take some water," Mr. Bennett said. The other man just smiled, shook his head, and went back to work.

"Me and mom brought white Powerade for you," Thomas said proudly.

Micah was approaching us by that point. I was mortified at the thought of him coming close to me looking the way I did, but there was nothing I could do about it.

"White Powerade, my favorite!" Micah said, reaching out to ruffle Thomas' hair. I could tell by the way he approached us that he thought we would all go back into the kitchen together, but he put a hand on Thomas' shoulder and looked at him with a concerned expression on our way inside. "You okay?" he asked, noticing his brother's red eyes.

Thomas stared at him as if he had no idea what Micah was talking about. "He was telling me about his favorite Bible verse," I explained.

Micah understood instantly and regarded me with a relived smile. "He's tenderhearted about the Bible."

"The Bible's Carly's favorite book too!" Thomas said.

Micah reached into the fridge, got a bottle of Powerade, and leaned against one of the counters as he unscrewed the lid and took a drink. He had shaggy brown hair that was damp with sweat and haphazardly held back by some sort of headband. I watched in awe as he chugged down half the bottle of his drink. I could see the muscles in his neck flex as he swallowed. He was dark complected, and beads of sweat ran down the side of his jaw and onto his neck. It was all I could do to keep my mouth from literally hanging open as I stared at him. He was a flawless human being, and I was completely mesmerized.

I glanced away for fear of being caught gawking. Thomas was preoccupied staring at the nozzle of the sink, no one else was in there, so I figured I hadn't been caught. By the time I looked back at Micah, he was done drinking. He set the bottle onto the counter and gave me an appraising smile. He had straight white teeth that were framed beautifully by full but masculine lips. I had to pull my eyes away from his lips so I wouldn't be the weirdo who stood there and stared at them.

I looked at his eyes instead. I hadn't seen his eyes when we were outside, but I could see them clearly now. They were an odd shade of green—a soft, greyish green that stood out in stark contrast to his dark complexion and strong features. They were so beautiful I got instantly uncomfortable looking at them and quickly shifted my gaze to the floor.

"So, the Bible's your favorite book?" he asked.

My eyes snapped up to find that he was regarding me with a sarcastic little half smile. I had no idea how to answer his question. All I wanted to do was make a good impression on him. I thought about telling him I had only said that for his brother's sake, but Thomas was standing right there and I didn't want to hurt his feelings.

"Thomas knows way more about the Bible than I do," I said, hoping that was a safe answer.

"Thomas knows more about the Bible than most preachers," Micah said.

"I don't know more than Pastor Dale," Thomas said, still messing with the nozzle of the sink.

"Where'd you go to school?" I heard Micah say. I turned to see that he was looking at me. I instinctually adjusted my ponytail and shifted my weight. Micah was so comfortable and confident leaning against the kitchen counter, and all I could do was stand there feeling nervous and tongue-tied.

I had to swallow hard before speaking so I could find my voice. "Warren," I said. "I still go there. I'm going into my senior year." I paused, but continued, "What about you?"

He crossed his legs and braced his weight on his arms. "I went to Reagan, but I'm at UT Austin now. I'm going into my sophomore year."

"Micah's in the band!" Thomas said, with his arms raised.

"Not the marching band," he said with a smirk. "I'm in the commercial music program."

"Like where you make commercials?" I asked, having no idea what he was talking about.

He let out a laugh like he thought my question was cute. "No, commercial music just means pop, rock, jazz, and so on—you know, anything besides classical. I'm also taking some business classes in case I end up going into construction like my dad."

"So what do you play?" I asked.

Micah started to tell me but then looked at Thomas. "Hey brother, can you please bring dad a bottled water from the fridge?"

"You were gonna bring it to him, but you started talking to Carly about music," Thomas said, looking back and forth between Micah and me. "I'll tell dad you're busy."

"I'll be out there in a second," Micah assured him. Thomas was looking in the fridge when Micah shifted his attention to me again. "I sing and play guitar and bass—mostly guitar though. I'm in two combos at school, but I'm in a band that keeps me really busy."

"What kind of music does your band play?"

He shrugged. "I don't really know how to classify it—alt rock would be the best way, I guess." He paused and looked me over. "Are you eighteen?" he asked.

I shook my head. "Not yet, why?"

"Because we're playing at Ramone's tonight. I was gonna tell you to come check us out. We're opening for The Miffs so there should be a good crowd."

I immediately started racking my brain to figure out how I could get into a bar. I would have to get a fake ID, which could possibly get me into even more trouble. I stared at his gorgeous green eyes—light green at the center with a thin dark green ring around the edge, and I said, "I didn't know The Miffs were playing! I hate to miss that. I could probably borrow a friend's license for the night if I decide to go."

"You know The Miffs?" he asked, looking impressed. Thank goodness I actually did. They were a popular local band and Gigi was into that sort of thing. She had turned me onto them last year.

I nodded. "I've never seen them live, though. That'd be cool."

He smiled and my heart felt like it wanted to melt. "It'd be cool if you could make it," he said. "My band's called Sweet East. We go on at 9."

Just then, a small group of volunteers came in through the front door. We both glanced that way. There were two guys and a girl. "Look who's relaxing on the job," one of the guys said.

Micah laughed. "I've been lifting seven hundred pound rocks all morning, chief. Looks like you haven't even broke a sweat."

"Oh, I'm sweating plenty. Your mom's a slave driver out there with those flowerbeds. How about I come over there and stick your pretty face in my armpits? Then you can tell me whether or not I've been sweating."

Micah laughed again. They were all about our age, and I could tell they were good friends by how they were messing around. Before I knew it, the whole rowdy group came into the kitchen. They were all talking at the same time and seemed very familiar with each other. I suddenly felt extremely out of place.

"I should get back to work," I said to Micah, as I turned to leave. "It was nice meeting you."

"Nice meeting you too, Carly."

I smiled. "Good luck with your show if I don't make it."

He lifted his chin at me with a smile. My comment set the rest of them off talking about the show that evening and how they all wanted to go. Thomas was still outside delivering the water to his dad, so I headed out of the kitchen and down the hallway by myself.

I stopped in the bathroom. The walls hadn't been painted, and the sink and tub fixtures still needed to be installed, but there was a mirror hanging over the sink. I locked the door and took a second to stare at myself. I breathed a long sigh, letting my shoulders slump. I'd been so nervous talking to Micah that it felt good to slouch for a second. I took the ponytail holder out of my hair and ran my hands through the tangled mess before putting it up again this time more neatly. I leaned in closer to the mirror to inspect my own eyes. They were hazel with touches of brown gold and green, but not nearly as striking as Micah's. He was so gorgeous and exotic looking that I seemed plain by comparison.

I stared at my reflection, wondering if someone like him could ever be attracted to someone like me. I felt embarrassed at the thought and wanted to splash water on my face, but couldn't since there was no faucet. I breathed another sigh as I headed back for the bedroom to look for my roller and grey paint. And there they were, right where I left them.

Joan was in her assumed position on the opposite wall from me. "Did you meet Micah?" she asked. I glanced back at her but she was still staring the other way painting.

"Yes ma'am," I said.

A few seconds passed, and I thought that was all she was going to say, but then she spoke again.

"He's not a baby, is he?"

I paused. "No ma'am," I said tentatively.

"He's handsome, isn't he?"

I glanced at the door to make sure no one was in the hall overhearing us. "I guess," I said in little more than a whisper.

I dipped the roller into the paint and picked up where I'd left off, making a long, grey stripe on the wall.

"They're a good family," she said.

I didn't know what to say to that, really. It seemed like she was just making conversation, but all I could think about was how I simply had to find a way into Ramone's that night.

"Yes ma'am, it seems that way," I said.

Joan didn't say any more. We painted for a few minutes in silence before she took another break leaving me in there alone. Thomas came in while she was gone. He was holding a purple t-shirt. It was one of the ones they had made for the volunteers. He insisted that I put it on right then, so I slipped it on over the one I was already wearing. It was purple with white lettering, and it had the words "Happy House" along with a child-like drawing of a house on the front. The back said "Volunteer Crew". Thomas was proud to say he'd been the one to come up with the name of the place, and the one who drew the t-shirt design. I told him I loved both.

He stayed in there for the next two hours talking to Joan and me while we painted. He told us about his fifteen year old sister, Emily, who would have been there helping today if she hadn't been away at cheerleading camp. After he told us all about Emily, he elaborated on Micah's musical endeavors, making me even more certain that I wanted to find a way to get into Ramone's to see for myself.

We talked the whole time we painted about things other than Jesus and the Bible, and he didn't cry once. He was funny and sweet, and I found myself charmed by his simple, positive outlook. I would have never dreamed I'd have such a great time talking to someone like Thomas. To my own surprise, I truly liked him—I felt like I'd hang out with him even if I weren't being forced to do so by my parents.

Chapter 4

I painted the art room, and later that afternoon, I moved to one of the bathrooms, which was being painted a light shade of blue. I ate a late lunch sometime in between the two projects. I met several new people and had a few good conversations throughout the day, but mostly I just stayed in my own little world where all I had to do was get paint from the bucket, to the roller, to the wall.

I saw Micah several more times during the day, but he was always in the middle of working or talking to someone else.

There really had been a lot of work done that day. There were 20 to 30 volunteers, and all of us worked continually. It was almost 6pm when I left, and the place looked entirely different than it did when I arrived that morning. I was maybe even a little bit proud to say I'd been a part of it.

Mrs. Bennett gave me a ride back to her house just before 6, and we barely made it there in time. I'd only been in their house for two or three minutes (barely long enough to inspect a few family pictures that were hanging on the wall) when Mike pulled up in the driveway. I was worried that if he came inside he would mention why I was there, so I thought it'd be best to meet him in the driveway.

"There's my stepdad," I said to Mrs. Bennett who was in the kitchen. Thomas and Micah, along with their dad were still at the Happy House finishing up a few last minute things, so she and I were the only ones there. "I'm gonna run out there and meet him so he doesn't have to get out of the truck," I called. "Thanks for having me!"

I could hear her footsteps as she came my way. I was standing by her front door when she made it in there, and she reached out to hug me. "Thank you so much for your hard work today, sweetheart," she said. "It warms my heart that so many young people came out to help."

I smiled, but couldn't help but feel a stab of guilt at her words. "I had fun," I said, honestly.

She smiled sweetly. "I'm so glad. And I know Thomas really loved having you there."

I opened the door quickly for fear that Mike would come inside. I caught him just in time. He'd already gotten out of the truck and was headed toward the front door. "Hey, you got one of my shirts!" he said with a huge smile on his face as I approached.

"Yep," I said, looking down at it. I wanted to stay mad him, but it had been a pretty good day and I just couldn't.

"How was it," he asked backing out of the driveway.

"They're actually a really neat family," I said.

He looked over the console at me with a huge grin. I wasn't looking at him, but I could see him wearing the oversized smile out of the corner my eye. "I told you," he said. "I knew you'd see the beauty of doing something like that."

"It doesn't change the fact that I think it's unfair to be punished for what happened last night," I said, holding my ground.

"Well that's for your mom and I to decide, and we just want what's best for you."

I sat quietly for a minute or so, deciding whether not I should argue about what was best for me. "The Bennett's son is in a band and he's playing music tonight," I said instead. "They asked if I wanted to go."

Mike's head whipped around to look at me. "Really?" he asked, before looking back at the road.

"Yeah. It doesn't start till 9 o'clock, though. I'd probably be out till midnight or so."

Normally that wouldn't be a big deal, but I figured I needed to ease him into it since I was punished. "You and mom took away my car and my phone. You didn't say anything about me having to stay home." Mike was quiet for long enough that I said, "They're a great family."

He sighed. "I'll have to talk to your mom, but I don't see why you can't go see some music tonight. Where's he playing, at a restaurant or something?"

"I've never been to the place, actually. It's called Ramone's." It was my best attempt at not having to lie while still concealing the truth. I figured my mom and Mike wouldn't do the research on what Ramone's actually was.

"Don't get your hopes up, but I'll talk to your mom about it when we get home.

I was already rejoicing on the inside.

"And I don't think either of us want you going anywhere with Gigi," he added.

"That's really unfair," I said, knowing she was my best bet at securing a fake ID. (Plus she loved The Miffs and would never forgive me if I went without her.) "Neither of us knew what was going on last night."

I looked at him and he shook his head in that parental way. "You can ask your mom, but don't be surprised she says no."

I did my best work that night, and ended up getting permission to go to the show. My mom wasn't happy about letting me go with Gigi, but somehow I made it happen. I think she and Mike were both pleasantly surprised with the fact that I came home in a good mood, so they were inclined to bend a little. They also let me use my phone for the evening in case we got in trouble and needed to call them.

Gigi had just turned 18, so she could use her own ID. She had an older sister named Ashley who was willing to let me use hers for the night since she was just hanging out with her boyfriend.

Gigi came over to my house at 8pm to finish getting ready and help me study Ashley's driver's license. "What's your sign?" she asked.

"What?"

"Your sign," she said. "Like Aries or whatever. It's a way they'll trick you to see if you're using a fake ID. You have to know Ashley's sign."

"I don't even know my own sign," I said. "I think I might be a Pieces."

"Well Ashley's not. You can't say you're a Pieces if they ask you that. They'll know it's not you."

"Well what is she?"

"I think she's a Sagittarius," she said.

I sighed. I was already nervous enough with seeing Micah again, much less using a fake ID and adding all this memorization to the mix. I almost called the whole thing off, but Gigi assured me everything would be all right.

We got dressed up for the occasion. I was a little bit of a tomboy, and my wardrobe reflected that, but Gigi help me put an outfit together, and I felt as confident as I could when we were done. I had on jeans with lots of holes and a tank top with a plaid button-up shirt over it. Gigi's outfit was a little more girly and revealing, and I made her put a shirt over it just till she got passed my parents. I also asked her to use her manners while we were talking to them, and she did a good job. She even apologized for everything that happened the night before. Mom and Mike were all smiles when we left.

We got to the bar at 10 till nine and there was a line. There was a guy at the door taking money and checking IDs. He had two sets of wristbands, pink ones for those under twenty-one, and green ones for those who were over. I only had $22 to my name, so I was surprised when we got close to the table and realized the cover charge was $15 a piece. I watched the people who went before me, feeling relieved that the guy didn't seem to be doing a thorough job of checking ID's, though.

That didn't stop me from being anxious. I was giddy with nervous anticipation the whole time we were standing in line. I had told Gigi all about Micah and how hot he was before we got there. She tried to bring it up again while we were waiting, but I told her to be quiet in case someone was standing there who knew him. I spotted a poster hanging on the wall that was promoting the event. The majority of it was a picture of The Miffs, but Sweet East was pictured at the bottom, and you could clearly see Micah standing front and center. I whispered to Gigi, and she checked it out. Her jaw hung open as she stared at the poster and then at me.

I giggled. "I told you," I said.

"The other guys in the band don't look bad either," she said. She wasn't whispering, and I glanced behind us again to make sure no one was paying attention.

We made it through the door with no hassle whatsoever. The guy seemed more interested in getting our $15 then he was at looking at our driver's license. He barely even glanced at it when I handed it to him, and I was sad I had taken all that time memorizing Ashley's stats.

"Come on, Ashley," Gigi said with a huge smile, after we paid. I rolled my eyes at her as we linked arms to make our way through the crowded bar to try to find a spot.

There were tables and chairs spread out all over the perimeter of the dance floor, but all of them were taken. A good bit of the dance floor was occupied with people standing around in groups. Gigi and I decided to get a soda from the bar so we'd have something to hold onto.

There was loud music playing, but it wasn't coming from the stage. The band's instruments were set up, but the stage was totally deserted. We got our sodas and found our way to a spot on the side of the dance floor. I figured we'd move out to the middle once the band came out, but for the time being, it felt good to be against the wall.

She and I made small talk, but all I could concentrate on was trying to locate Micah Bennett. I had no luck with that. After several minutes of looking around the place I gave up and figured he was in the back somewhere.

It was 9:15 when someone came out onto the stage. It was a guy dressed in all black. Several people in the crowd yelled out when he used his hand to tap the microphone a few times to see if it was working.

"How's everybody doing tonight?" he asked, and a whole round of cheers followed.

Everyone who had been standing around the perimeter of the dance floor began making their way toward the stage, and Gigi and I followed.

"You guys stoked to see The Miffs?" he yelled.

He stuck his microphone out over the crowd to pick up our yells, but we didn't need it. Everyone clapped, screamed, and whistled so loudly it made me giggle and want to use my fingers to plug up my ears. Gigi and I looked at each other, laughing at all the ruckus.

"First we have a special treat for you guys! Straight out of Austin, Texas... let's hear it for Sweet East!"

The crowd erupted again, and he left the stage as Micah's four-piece band made their way out there. Micah found his place at the microphone and bent down to strap the guitar onto his shoulder. I started wiggling and jiggling from side to side with excitement. I didn't even realize I was pinching Gigi until she said, "Ouch!"

"I'm sorry," I said. "But isn't he the hottest thing you've ever seen?"

Gigi looked back at the stage and considered it seriously. She cocked her head to the side and really took a good look. "I think he is, actually," she said in all seriousness. That made me start giggling again.

With a pick in his hand, he grabbed the top of the microphone and adjusted it to his liking. He was smiling as he did it, and I could hear girls let out whoops and hollers randomly.

"I assume everybody's feeling good this fine Saturday night," he said, still smiling. Another round of cheers and whistles. "We're Sweet East, and this first song's called Way Down Low."

With that, he let go of the mic, and turned to nod at the band before making the first strum of the guitar.

I couldn't believe my ears. I instantly had a new favorite band. I loved the style of their music, and his voice. He had a perfect voice to match his perfect face. He was officially perfect. There was something about a guy who could sing, and singing was something Micah Bennett did well. He smiled as he performed, and he never ever missed a note. He moved around the stage, interacting with his band mates during the times he wasn't singing. I loved everything about his stage presence, and so did the rest of the crowd. Everyone's attention was focused on the stage as they danced and swayed to the music.

I don't know how many songs they played, maybe eight or so. I was too transfixed to count. I didn't want the set to end. I had absolutely no interest in seeing The Miffs. "Can you believe how good they were?" Gigi said, as they left the stage.

I shook my head, looking stunned, which cracked her up. "I had no idea what to expect," I said. "I can't believe they're opening for The Miffs in a place like this. They should be famous."

She shrugged and raised her eyebrows at me. "Maybe they will get famous," she said. "Then you can marry a rock star."

I was about to make a joke about being married to a famous guy when I saw something that turned my wonderful evening a terrible one. The members of Sweet East were exiting a door on the far side of the stage. I caught sight of them since no one else was standing over there. Micah was the first one out, and I smiled for a second thinking I'd finally have the chance to talk to him. But then, out of nowhere, a blonde girl ran up to him. I watched as she threw herself into his arms.

I had to swallow to keep my throat from closing up completely. I kept watching, hoping he would push her off like some sort of unwanted, pesky fan, but he didn't. He smiled and bent to kiss her. It wasn't just a quick peck on the lips; it was a real kiss—one that lasted long enough that the rest of his band walked around them, leaving him behind.

Chapter 5

I stared at Micah and the blonde for several long, horrible seconds before Gigi, who was standing next to me, realized what I was gawking at.

"Ohh," I heard her say from beside me. I could tell by the way she said it that she knew I'd be disappointed at the sight.

"Let's go," I said, feeling humiliated. I peeled my eyes off the happy couple and turned to face Gigi.

She was looking at me like I was out of my mind. "Did you say let's go?"

"Yeah, let's get out of here."

Her brow furrowed as she smirked at me. "We haven't even seen The Miffs... the band who we just paid 15 dollars to see."

"Not me," I said. I glanced around to make sure no one in the crowd was listening to me, and then I pointed in the direction of Micah and the blonde.

"I'm not gonna stay and watch that all night."

She let out a little laugh. "Then don't look at them," she said, as if that was obvious.

"You can't seriously think we're gonna stay," I said.

"You can't seriously think we're gonna leave," she replied. "We paid to see The Miffs."

"Gigi, please," I pleaded.

She stared at me trying to figure out how in the world I was so affected by a guy I had only met earlier that day. "Carly, I wish you could step outside yourself and see that this really isn't a big deal. It's not like he's going to come over here and laugh at you for coming. If you end up talking to him tonight we'll just act like we're here to see The Miffs, which we are!"

"I'm definitely not going to talk to him tonight," I said, disappointment evident in my tone.

She cocked her head and stared into my eyes, searching for truth. "Did he lead you to believe he wanted to be with you tonight?"

I could tell she was being protective of me. I shook my head. "No," I insisted sadly. "I guess I was just hoping…" I trailed off, shaking my head. "It's stupid." I let out a defeated sigh and she put her hand on my arm.

"What's stupid is if you let this little hiccup ruin our night." She patted me on the arm and smiled, trying to get me to smile too. "Seriously, Carly, there are so many hot guys here tonight—just look around! Don't get all bummed out just because one of them's taken."

I wanted to tell her he was the only one I was interested in, and it was pointless for me to try to look at anyone else, but instead I faked a little smile. She was extremely excited to see The Miffs, and what sort of friend would I be if I didn't let her do that after she'd helped me find a way in.

"Atta girl," she said, capitalizing on my forced smile.

I lost Micah in the crowd, thank goodness. Gigi and I saw a few guys we recognized, and went over to talk to them before The Miffs took the stage. They had all graduated from our high school in the spring and were the artsy, theater types. Gigi and I didn't know them very well, but when you saw someone you even slightly recognized in a place like that, you tend to talk to them.

There were five of them in the group, and they had one of the highly sought after tables. It was a high-top table with three barstools. Everyone who didn't have a place to sit just sort of gathered around standing. They'd all seen The Miffs several other times, and we listened as they talked about their previous concert experiences. One of them knew one of the guys in the band, and he bragged about partying with them after one of their shows.

I really didn't care about all of their stories. I really didn't care about The Miffs at all. It was silly, but I honestly thought this night would end with me in Micah's arms—or with me talking to him and exchanging phone numbers. Either way, I did not expect the blonde, and that was a bitter pill to swallow.

"Heyyy, you made it," I heard from over my shoulder. My gut clinched instantly but I didn't turn around. Then I felt a tap on my shoulder. "You're Carly right?" I knew it was Micah. I turned to face him with as much confidence as I could muster.

"Oh, hey!" I said seeming surprised.

Yep, just as I thought, he was standing there with the gorgeous blonde at his side—both of them smiling. I didn't know which one of them to look at. My gaze shifted nervously between the two. *Smile Carly, smile.* She was a size two beauty pageant type with big, perfectly styled hair that cascaded over her tiny shoulders. She had on a lot of exquisitely applied make up. She was a head-turner. *Just keep smiling.*

They stood next to each other, and Micah had his arm casually draped around her waist. "Carly, this is my girlfriend Sophia." He looked down at Sophia the Perfect with a smile. "Carly came to help out at the Happy House today."

"Aw, I'm so sorry I missed that," she said. "I had some things to take care of in Austin today with my sorority."

Of course she did.

She glanced up at Micah. "Is this the one Thomas was talking about?"

Micah laughed and nodded. "My brother *loves* you," he said smiling at me. "He was talking about you all through dinner,"

"You must have made quite the impression," Sophia chimed in.

I smiled as sincerely as I could, but all I could think was that I had made the impression on the wrong brother. "I really liked Thomas," I said. "I had fun getting to know him today."

"Isn't he adorable?" Sophia said with a huge smile. Micah gave her a little squeeze, and she glanced up at him. They exchanged a brief smile and then, to my horror, a kiss.

I seriously wanted to run for the door. I couldn't look at her anymore after that. I decided to focus my attention on Micah for the remainder of the conversation, which I hoped would be short. The guy knew how to dress. That was one of the things that made him stand out. In a sea of guys who didn't know how to pick clothes that were stylish and fit them well, Micah looked like a fashion model who'd been dressed by a stylist. I followed the lines of his perfectly fitted jeans, trying not to make it obvious that I was completely infatuated.

"We liked your band," Gigi said from beside me. I forgot she was even there, but I was grateful for the distraction.

Micah smiled and extended a hand to shake hers. "Thanks," he said. "Are you one of Carly's friends?"

"Yep, I'm Gigi," she said, shaking his hand. "I was planning on dragging Carly out to see The Miffs tonight, but it was cool that she ran into you today. It worked out that we could come a little early and support Thomas' brother."

"Good, I'm glad you guys made it out," he said. He glanced at the guys sitting at the table, and Gigi proceeded to introduce all of them as if we were good friends and had been there with them the whole time. I was so thankful for her intervention during the whole exchange that I wanted to just reach right out and hug her. She basically took over and made it seem like Micah was not the main objective of me being there, which was entirely untrue.

Micah and his girlfriend were only at our table for a few minutes, but it seemed like a lifetime since all I could do was think about how I'd never have him. The Miffs took the stage not long after they left, and I focused my attention on other things.

Zeke Ramirez happened to be that other thing.

He was one of the guys sitting at our table. I hadn't even noticed him in that way before Micah and his girlfriend came over, but I was so agitated afterwards that Zeke just kept getting cuter and cuter as the night went on. He had dark hair and eyes and wore dark clothes that fit his whole look. He had that dangerous vibe going on, and with the way I was feeling reckless, he was just what the doctor ordered. We didn't hang with the same crowd in high school, so I'd never really gotten to know him. I figured there was no time like the present to give it a shot, even if it didn't amount to anything in the long run.

Gigi was busy listening to the band and talking to Chase, one of the other guys at the table, so I stood next to Zeke. We talked about going to school at Warren and some of our favorite and least favorite teachers there. He had a fairly solemn demeanor, but several times during our conversation, he cracked a smile. It made his face handsome, and it made me feel good—like I'd earned it since he didn't offer them freely.

"What are your plans for the fall?" I asked.

"I think I'll take a semester or two off, but I want to study theatre. I'll probably go to San Antonio College to start."

"That's cool," I said.

He shrugged. "It's not Juilliard."

"Well, it's a start—like you said."

He gave me an almost imperceptible smile. "What about you?"

"I still have another year at Warren," I said.

"And after that?"

I smiled shyly. "It's pretty dorky compared to theatre."

"Accounting?" he asked with another hint of a smile.

"Close. Just as dorky."

"Science?"

A smile spread across my face. "Yeah. I'm not a genius or anything, but it's the only subject I really like."

"So you're gonna be a scientist?"

"No. I don't know." I shrugged. "I don't really have a plan yet. All I know is that it's my favorite subject. I might end up being a teacher or something. I'm hoping they'll help me figure that out once I go to college."

He reached up to the side of my face and tucked a strand of loose hair behind my ear. "None of us have it all figured out," he said.

It felt good to have him pay attention to me. Maybe the spark wasn't as significant as it had been with Micah, but Zeke was nice, he seemed to like me, and best of all, he didn't come with a blonde.

"See? I told you we should stay," Gigi said on our way home. "Aren't you glad we didn't leave?"

"You might have been right," I admitted. I was in the middle of texting my mom to let her know the show was over and we were on our way home.

"Who are you texting, Zeke?" she asked.

"No. I'm texting my mom."

"I saw you two exchange numbers," she said, taking her eyes off the road to glance at me.

"He's nice. We'll probably try to hang out sometime." I poked her arm. "I saw you talking to Chase."

She giggled. "He's cute isn't he? It's cool that they're friends. We can all go out together."

I smiled and agreed with her, but I couldn't quite get the sting of disappointment to go away.

"You'll get over that singer," she said, sensing my withdrawal. "Give yourself two dates with Zeke, and you'll forget that other guy ever existed."

She had to be right. There were plenty of famous musicians and actors in the world whom I would love to go out with, and I didn't care whether or not they had girlfriends. I wasn't the type of girl to spend my life pining away on someone I'd never have. I knew it was just a waste of time. All I had to do was put Micah Bennett in the same category as those other guys—the untouchables. The sooner I came to terms with that, the better.

Chapter 6

Five years later.

"Zeke?" I called, opening his front door.

He hadn't returned my texts all afternoon. I knew he was home. I'd seen his car in the driveway.

"Zeke?" I said a little louder.

His tiny house was dark and cluttered. There was trash and piles of clothes strewn out all over the place, and to top it all off, it smelled terrible. *What was that stench?* I covered my nose and mouth with a hand as I tiptoed through his disaster of a living room.

"Zeke?" I repeated.

I had a gut-wrenching feeling something was wrong. Dread and fear began to flood my body. I had a distinct feeling that he was home, and yet he wouldn't answer me.

"Zeke!" I yelled in a frustrated tone. "Where are you?" I peeked into the tiny kitchen. "Stop messing around, you're scaring me!"

It was an itty-bitty, two bedroom house. I'd been there tons of times, but somehow it seemed unfamiliar. I peered into the extra bedroom, which Zeke used for his art stuff. He was a singer, a poet, a painter, and an actor—and this room housed many of the supplies he used. I usually loved Zeke's art, but even this room seemed dismal and eerie as I looked inside.

"Zeke!" I called, feeling jumpy and on edge.

From my vantage point in the small hallway, I could see into his tiny, dated bathroom and partially into his bedroom. Something told me I'd find him in his bedroom. He was probably sleeping. He'd been drinking lately, and was likely passed out.

"Zeke, your house is a mess!" I called. I tested my luck with uncovering my nose but realized it still stank and quickly covered it again.

I stepped into his bedroom feeling certain I would find him in there. My heart sank as I stared at his empty double bed. There were windows on the far side of the room but heavy curtains covered them, making it really dark. I decided to open the windows and let a little bit of light and fresh air into the place. It was disgusting, and I felt a strong urge to clean. I vaguely wondered why I was even dating a guy who lived in such a messy place. I walked around the foot of the bed to the other side of the room and pushed open the heavy fabric covering the window. Sunlight spilled in, making me squint and glance downward.

And there he was—what was left of him anyway. I instantly covered my mouth again and gaged as I tried to focus on the figure that lie on the floor on the far side of his bed. Panic flooded my body. I wanted to run, scream, do something... but fear had an iron grip on me, and I was completely paralyzed. I just stood there and stared down at his lifeless body for several long seconds. I should have looked away, but I couldn't. I stayed completely motionless, like a stone statue.

There was no question he was dead. The top half of his head was completely blown away. All I could see was mangled flesh and blood.

The fear.

The dread.

The crippling grip it had on me was too much to handle. It was the most disturbing image I'd ever seen. I tried to scream, but it came out more like a moan.

I couldn't move. All I could do was look at what used to be my boyfriend. I tried to scream again, and again it was a moan. I could see myself moving and screaming. I could see my body doing it, but I knew I was paralyzed—unable to move or even make a noise.

And then I did it.

I made one final gut-wrenching push, and it was over.

I was out of there.

My eyes opened, and I awoke from the dream, staring at the ceiling of my own bedroom. My heart was pounding, and I was struggling to catch my breath.

A cold sweat had come to the surface of my entire body. I stayed there, completely motionless for several long seconds before I picked my head up to glance around.

It had only been a nightmare. I was in my own bed in my own room. My shaggy, brown dog was lying flat on his back next to me and I reached out and put my hand on his warm belly just to try to get some sense of comfort and peace.

He stirred a little at my touch, but didn't wake up. I reached onto my nightstand with the other hand and picked up my phone to check the time.

"Two A.M.," I whispered before letting my head hit the pillow again.

My body was so wound up from the nightmare that it took a good fifteen or twenty minutes for my heart rate to slow down afterward. I was so relieved to have Roscoe lying next to me in the bed. Waking up with a nightmare was never easy, but having him next to me helped the aftermath. It took me three hours to fall back asleep.

The next day was Sunday, so thankfully I didn't have to work. I had plans to have coffee at 10am with a friend of mine named Trish, and I showed up looking as tired and frustrated as I felt. I saw her through the window as I approached, and she told me with hand gestures that I should just come to the couch where she was sitting because she already had my coffee.

"What's the matter?" was the first thing out of her mouth when I got close enough to hear her.

I sat on the couch with a huff, not even bothering to take the bag off of my shoulder. "What'd you get me?" I asked, sitting up to grab the paper cup off the coffee table.

"A vanilla latte. What's up with you?"

"The dream."

"Again?"

I took a small sip of coffee, set it down, and rubbed my face with my hands. "Thanks for that. It's good." I sighed. "Yeah, same dream." I sat back again, still feeling disturbed and restless. "It's been two months since the last one, though."

She smiled. "That's a good thing."

I managed a half smile. "I guess."

She studied me as if I was a puzzle she could put back together. "Was it exactly like..." she started to ask.

"Yes. It was exactly like it happened in real life," I said. "Only in the dream, his house was different— it was gross and dark. I was scared even before I saw him."

I started dating Zeke when I was seventeen years old and he was eighteen. We dated for a year before he committed suicide. He worked at a music store in the mall during the year we were dating and had plans to start college with me. He said we'd be freshmen together.

His depression came on quickly. He always wrote a lot of poetry, but during the summer when we celebrated our one-year anniversary, his poems took a melancholy turn. He began acting like he changed his mind about going to college saying he would never amount to anything anyway. I knew he was sad, but I had absolutely no idea he was capable of doing what he did. He took his own life in the bedroom of his parents' house, and since they were at work, I'd been the one to find him.

No one should ever, I repeat EVER have to see anything like that. It had been four years since I found him, and I still resented him for making me look at that. Imagine if it had been his mom.

Trish put her hand on my leg and let out a long sigh. She had no idea what to say, and I couldn't blame her for that. "Do you think you should try those pills?"

"I'm not going to get on pills for the rest of my life. The nightmares are getting farther and farther apart, and I'm able to live a pretty normal life in spite of them. I'm not gonna subject myself to a lifetime of prescriptions to help me get over it." I shrugged. "People see things in life that suck. I should be able to get over it by myself."

"Have you seen a therapist?"

I glanced at her. "Who do you think gave me the pills?"

"Did it help you to talk about it?"

"It helped a little, I guess. No amount of talking can remove the memory, though."

I took another sip of my coffee and stared blankly at the chair in front of me. It was the first brisk day of fall, and I had on a tank top and a loose, grey sweatshirt with a huge open neck that hung off of my shoulder. I knew I looked like a mess, and I was thankful that Trish didn't care. She and I met a year ago when we were doing our student teaching at the same high school and had hit it off instantly. We were both in our first year of teaching now, but at different schools. I was teaching physical science at Roosevelt High, and she taught English at Reagan.

"It might be a bad day to tell you this," she said, "but one of my roommates just told us she's moving out in a few weeks. She's going to live with her boyfriend."

I was still living with my mom and stepdad. I was 22 now and well aware of the fact that I should probably look for a place of my own—especially now that I had a real job. Moving in with Trish wouldn't be a bad option, actually. She lived in a 4-bedroom house with three roommates. I definitely wasn't ready to live in a house by myself. I wasn't sure if I'd ever be.

"What about Roscoe?" I asked.

"None of us have dogs, but I don't think the landlord would care. He's potty trained, right?"

I nodded.

"I'm sure you'd have to pay a pet deposit or something. I'd have to look at the lease."

"Would your other roommates mind?"

She shook her head. "I don't think so."

"How much is rent?"

"Six fifty, but the bedroom you'd have has its own bathroom."

I loved her house. It was in a great neighborhood. I loved her roommates for that matter. I knew it was Brittany who was moving out to live with her boyfriend, because her other two roommates were guys. I'd met them both several times and liked them a lot.

I was relieved to have something else to think about besides the dream. "Do you mind if I think about it for a day?"

"Not at all," she said. "We're not going to put an ad out or anything. If you don't want it, Ryan and Isaac both said they know someone to ask."

"Don't let them ask just yet," I said. "I think I might want it. I just need a day to think about it."

I relaxed onto the couch with my cup of coffee and took a few sips.

"Just think about paramedics, and cops, and doctors," she said, obviously still concerned about my dream. "Think about all the messed up stuff they have to see every day." She paused and shook her head absentmindedly. "They must get immune to it."

"That's why I'm a teacher," I said. "I can't imagine getting confronted with tragedy every day. I wouldn't be able to leave the house. I don't know how they do it."

In the four years since it happened, the trauma had decreased significantly. I went to college, got a job, and lived a somewhat normal life. It was mornings like this that were hard.

The dream was even more disturbing than the reality had been, and it always made the memory so fresh in my mind. "I'll be fine," I said. "Who knows, maybe last night was the last time I have that dream."

"Maybe so," she said with a smile. "Maybe your new bedroom will only allow sweet dreams."

I started to ask what she meant by new bedroom but then realized she was talking about the one at her house. I smiled.

"Excuse me, did you volunteer at the Happy House?" I heard a woman's voice say from my right side. Her voice was soft and tentative, and I assumed she wasn't talking to me, but somewhere in the back of my mind I registered *Happy House*. I knew I'd heard that somewhere before. I glanced in her direction and noticed a lady sitting at a table, swiveling in her chair to face me. She had a familiar smile. Wait. She was Claire Bennett.

A flood of memories washed over me as I looked at her. I must have been staring blankly because she said, "Are you Mike Murphy's daughter?"

I managed a smile and a nod. "Step daughter, yes."

"I'm—"

I cut her off. "Mrs. Bennett. I remember you."

"It's so good to see you," she said. "How have you been?"

"Great," I said, which was only a little lie.

"Thomas is going to be thrilled to see you. He talked about you for months after you helped out that day."

"Is he here?" I asked, looking around. "He's with his sister at the counter getting our food."

She gave me a huge, goofy smile. "I'm the official table saver."

I felt like I was in the twilight zone, but somehow managed to remember to introduce Trish. They were greeting each other when Thomas and his little sister Emily walked up carrying trays. I thought of her as 15 because Thomas told me that's how old his little sister was, but obviously time had passed. She was a beautiful girl who was, if my first grade math was correct, 20 now.

"Thomas, look who it is!" Mrs. Bennett said. I didn't want her to put him on the spot. I knew there was no way he would remember me after such a long time. I unfolded my legs and stood up with every intention of reintroducing myself.

"Carlyyyy!" he said. He was holding a tray with a sandwich, and he raised it over his head in his usual greeting.

"Be careful, Thomas. Watch your food," Emily said cringing up at the tray. He quickly set it on the table in front of his mom and crossed over to me with his arms held open wide.

He hugged me with such love and relief it was as if I was a long lost friend—someone he'd been waiting desperately to see again. I was already on edge emotionally, and there was such love in his embrace that tears rose to my eyes. I tried to hold them back but I couldn't. I blinked hard, trying to clear my vision.

Chapter 7

When Thomas finally let me go, I bent to get my coffee so it wouldn't be so obvious that I was feeling overwhelmed. I had to swallow hard and clear my throat before I could speak. I stood up with my coffee in my hand and a huge smile on my face. Mrs. Bennett and Emily were busy getting the food situated on the table, but Thomas just stood there staring at me.

"You don't look the same," he said. I ran a hand through my hair nervously.

"Well, it's been a few years, hasn't it, Thomas?" Mrs. Bennett chimed in, still distracted by the food on her table. Then, her head came up to regard me. "Have you met Emily?"

"No ma'am," I said. I looked at Emily. "I think you were away at camp the day I met the rest of your family."

"It was when we had that work party getting the house ready," Mrs. Bennett said.

Emily made a regretful face like she had no idea what we were talking about.

"I think it was cheerleading camp," I said.

Emily smiled and nodded even though I was pretty sure she still didn't remember. She stepped towards me, extending her hand. She had on a stylish sweater with leggings and boots. A scarf and several necklaces tied the whole thing together. I looked like a big couch potato compared to her. The thought made me adjust my hair again before I shook her hand.

"Emily," she said smiling.

"Carly," I replied.

Claire glanced our way. "Emily's studying English at San Antonio College."

"That's what I did," Trish said from her spot on the couch.

"No kidding!" Emily said, smiling at her. "Are you done?"

Trish nodded. "I'm teaching at Reagan now."

"That was my high school," Emily said.

Trish smiled. "I took Mrs. Henderson's place."

"That old coot finally retired?" Emily asked laughing.

"Emily Nicole!" Mrs. Bennett scolded, looking up from her food.

"It's okay," Trish said, craning her neck so she could see past me to Mrs. Bennett. "She was like six hundred years old when she retired. She even called herself an old coot."

Emily and Trish both giggled, but my attention was focused on Thomas who was staring at me intently. He almost seemed sad.

"You didn't come to the Happy House for a long time," he said. "Where'd you go?"

"I knowww, I need to come see you guys, don't I?"

"Today?" he asked, in all seriousness.

Emily took her spot at the table across from her mom, but Thomas stood next to me. I stammered, wondering what to say or if he was serious.

"We're not going to be there today, Thomas," Mrs. Bennett said. "Remember?"

"Tomorrow?" Thomas asked. He stared at me, waiting for my answer.

"Tomorrow's Sunday, Thomas. The house is closed," Mrs. Bennett said.

"When are you coming?" he asked, not taking his eyes off me.

"I didn't get to meet you yet," Trish said.

I could tell she was trying to give me some time to figure out a way to gracefully get out of doing whatever Thomas was asking. I was thankful she was nice enough to intervene, but part of me wanted to check out the house and was glad Thomas was excited to have me back.

"My name is Thomas Gabriel Bennett," Thomas said to her, shaking her hand. "Are you friends with Carly?"

"I sure am," Trish said. "We were teachers at the same school last year."

Thomas looked straight at me as Trish sat back onto the couch. "You're a teacher?" he asked.

"Yep."

Mrs. Bennett had a mouth full of food, but she looked up from her table. Using a napkin to cover her mouth when she spoke, she said, "Where do you teach?"

"I teach science at Roosevelt."

"You teach science experience?" Thomas asked.

"It's ex-peri-ments," Emily corrected.

"I teach experience too," I said, winking at Thomas. "They're very similar."

"Can you show me something?" he asked, a look of excitement washing over his face.

"Oh, that's an excellent idea," Mrs. Bennett said. "If you ever wanted to volunteer, I'm sure everyone at the house would love to watch a science experiment."

Thomas began clapping his hands. He was so excited at the thought that there was absolutely no way I could deny him.

"Of course," I said. "I'd love to come by and talk science sometime."

"Today?" Thomas asked. He looked at his mom who was leveling him with a look that said he knew better. "Oh, yeah, not today," he said, smiling.

Mrs. Bennett reached onto the back of her chair and began digging in her purse. She pulled out a business card with the contact information for the Happy House written on it. She handed it to me before quickly changing her mind and asking for it back. She pulled out a pen and wrote something on the back of it. "This is my cell," she said. "Maybe we can set up a time for next week or the one after."

Thomas sighed as if that seemed like an eternity. I couldn't help myself. I reached out to hug him again. It made me feel so good that he was excited to see me, especially after what a long night I had.

Mrs. Bennett gave a little smile at the sight of us hugging, but continued, "We have arts and crafts Monday, Wednesday, and Friday at 4pm. We always have a good turnout for that. Maybe you could do something right afterwards at around 5. I'm sure a lot of people would stay for a science experience." She winked at Thomas who still had his arm around my shoulder.

"When are you coming?" Thomas asked pulling back to look at me.

"I'm not sure yet, but it'll be soon. I'll call your mom and set up a time."

"You look different," he repeated, staring at me.

I smiled. "You look different too. You got a haircut."

Thomas touched the side of his head. "Yeah, I got a haircut."

"You need to come eat your lunch, Thomas," Mrs. Bennett said. "Emily and I are going to be done before you even start.

"We saw Carly here!" he said, squeezing my shoulder again.

"I'm glad I saw you too, Thomas," I said, leaning over to give him a quick kiss on the cheek. "You made my day."

He looked at me like he wasn't quite sure what the phrase meant.

"Come eat and let Carly get back to her coffee," Mrs. Bennett reminded him.

He nodded and hugged me again. He held onto me as I pulled back, seeming reluctant to break contact.

"I'll see you soon, I promise," I assured him.

He nodded and went to the table to join his mom and sister. Trish and I settled in on the couch and had a whispered conversation about work and the possibility of me moving in with her until the Bennetts left. I stood up to hug them all again when they said goodbye and promised Thomas that I'd be seeing him soon.

"How'd you know them?" Trish said when they left. They had been sitting close enough that she hadn't dared ask that question earlier.

"I got in trouble the summer before my senior year of high school and my parents made me do a day of community service at this house the Bennetts built. It's a gathering place for people with disabilities—somewhere for them to go to just have fun and hang out. Anyway, they were finishing it up, and they had a volunteer workday. I painted a bedroom and a bathroom. It's called the Happy House. Thomas named it."

"Where is it?" she asked.

"Over in Stone Oak—not too far from Reagan."

"That's cool," she said. "They seem like a nice family."

"They are," I said. I sighed and stared straight ahead, lost in thought my few seconds.

"What?" she asked.

A smile touched my lips. "I had a huge crush on their other son for all of one day."

"A one day crush? That's not very long."

"Yeah, it was just until I found out that he was already taken by a perfect little blonde sorority girl."

"What's his name?" she asked.

I got lost in thought again, remembering how it happened. "Micah," I said wistfully. "The day I had a crush on him was the same day I met Zeke."

"Zeke from the dream?"

I smiled and rolled my eyes at her knowing she knew there was no other Zeke in my life.

"I knew Zeke a little from high school since we both went to Warren, but I didn't really talk to him until the night I went to a bar to watch Micah's band play. I figured out he had a girlfriend, and I started talking to Zeke."

"So Zeke was a rebound?" she asked.

I chuckled. "I don't know if you can call it a rebound since nothing ever existed between me and Micah."

"So let me get this straight. You met Micah when you were punished and had to do community service. You fell in love and went to go see his band play at a bar. That's where the sorority girl showed up, so you forgot about Micah and started dating Zeke."

73

"That's about right, except for the me falling in love part. Infatuation was more like it. But it was impossible not to be infatuated with him. He was the singer in a band, and his face looked like the definition of perfect."

"So, what's he doing now?" she asked.

I glanced at her like she had lost her mind. "How am I supposed to know that? I never saw him again after that night at the bar. He's probably married with kids by now."

Her brows furrowed. "How old is he?"

I shrugged. "Probably a couple of years older than me," I said, as if details about him weren't etched into my memory.

"I'm sure he's not married," she said.

"It doesn't really matter."

"Sure it does. What if you run into him when you go to teach that class next week?"

"I won't," I said. I knew that wouldn't happen. I had written him off years ago. "Micah Bennett was the furthest thing in my mind when I agreed to volunteer."

Okay, so if I'm being entirely honest, maybe he wasn't the *furthest* thing from my mind. But I knew in my heart it would never amount to anything, so whatever thoughts I had about him didn't really count.

"I like Thomas," I said, honestly. "The only reason I agreed to do the class was for him."

"Yeah, but it might be a bonus if you got to hang out with his big brother a little bit," Trish said, raising her eyebrows.

"Micah's the little brother," I said. "Thomas is older than him."

"Really?" she asked.

I nodded.

"He's definitely not married with kids," she said, narrowing her eyes at me.

I laughed. "Stop."

"Stop what?"

"Stop acting like something could happen. You're just gonna make me get my hopes up and he's an untouchable."

"What's that mean?"

"It means, he's untouchable, just like it sounds. He's like Liam Hemsworth, Channing Tatum, Ryan Gossling, Chris Evans... you get the picture."

"Do they need someone to volunteer to teach an English class at this house?" she asked with wide eyes.

I giggled and slapped her leg.

"I think you should get dressed for the occasion just in case he's there," she said. "You haven't gone out with anyone since I've known you. It's about time you start dating."

I let out a defeated sigh and shook my head. I thought about all the baggage I was stuck carrying around with me thanks to Zeke.

"Don't start with the poor me crap," she said, seeing me looking hopeless.

"What? Nobody should have to see what I saw."

"You're absolutely right, Carly. Nobody should have to see that. It sucks. What he did was selfish, and now you're stuck with the repercussions of it. But you know what? Get over it. Everybody has seen some crappy stuff in their life. Imagine cops who have to see that stuff all the time."

"Yeah, but it's not their boyfriend."

"Maybe sometimes it is. You think you're the only one who's ever found someone they loved who committed suicide? There's probably a whole support group online for people like you."

"I'm not trying to be dramatic or complain," I said feeling somewhat ashamed. "It's just fresh in my mind since I had the dream and everything."

"I'm not saying it doesn't suck. I'm sure it does. I hate it for you that you had to see that, and it's terrible that it sticks with you for so long. I just don't want to see you pass up the opportunity to meet someone new."

"I'll just start with teaching the class," I said. "If Thomas' ultra hot, untouchable baby brother happens to be there, then great. If not, then that's great too."

"That's right," she said. "But it won't hurt to put on a little lip-gloss just in case."

Chapter 8

I made arrangements with Mrs. Bennett to go to the Happy House the following Wednesday afternoon at 5. She made sure to tell me not to stress about bringing complicated materials. She said they'd enjoy just about anything, even something on an elementary level.

I asked her if Thomas had ever seen the Mentos and Coke experiment, and she said he hadn't, so that's what I decided to bring. She asked if she could bring anything to help me out and I told her a couple of sawhorses and a long piece of wood might come in handy, but it wasn't necessary. She said she would see what Jesse could dig up in the garage.

I had a tarp and safety goggles in my classroom, so all I needed to buy was the soda and Mentos. I was excited about doing it. It was a crowd-pleasing experiment, and I had a feeling Thomas would really get a kick out of it.

It was ten till five when I pulled up that Wednesday afternoon. I barely recognized the house. It was amazing what five years of life could change. The landscaping was filled in with beautiful flowers and there was a nice stone sign in the yard with the name of the place and a picture of Thomas' house design etched into it.

I had 6 two-liter bottles of soda in my trunk, but I decided to leave them in there until I knew they were ready for me. Jesse Bennett was standing on the porch. I hadn't seen him at first, and he kind of startled me. "Oh, hi Mr. Bennett," I said, holding a hand to my chest.

He chuckled a little. "Hey Carly, how are you?"

"I'm good," I said. I reached out to shake his hand and he pulled me in for a hug.

He looked exactly the same, other than maybe a few extra gray hairs. He had the same smiling eyes that made me feel right at home.

"Thanks for coming today," he said. "Thomas is fit to be tied in there."

"Aw, is he excited?"

Mr. Bennett shook his head and laughed a little. "He's been asking for days if it's Wednesday yet."

I smiled. "I'm so glad to hear that. I'm excited too."

He put his hand on my shoulder and looked down at me appraisingly. "So you went and became a science teacher, huh?"

"Yes sir. I'm in my first year at Roosevelt."

"We'll have to see if we can get you on at Reagan," he said. "Go Rattlers!"

I laughed. "I'd love to get on at Reagan. I have a good friend who teaches English there, and next month I'll be moving into a house close by."

"Oh, you got a house in the neighborhood?" he asked.

"I'm just renting," I said. "I'll be roommates with the girl I was just talking about, my teacher friend."

He patted my shoulder. "Well that sounds good. You'll be close by. Maybe you can come by here more often. I know Thomas would love it."

"Maybe so," I said.

He looked at my car. "Can I help you with your supplies? I brought the sawhorses you asked for. I didn't know what kind of board you needed, so I brought a few options."

"I just need a long board to line up the sodas," I said. "Like 10 or 12 inches by 6 feet or so would be great, but anything will work, really. I can do it on the ground if I need to."

He smiled. "No, I have something that'll work."

We took the next five minutes to set up the experiment in the backyard. I put a tarp on the ground and we placed a board on top two sawhorses. I put a second tarp over his board since I didn't want to get it sticky. He helped me carry the two-liter bottles to the backyard, and I lined them up on the board. "That's all," I said once I had them situated.

He gave me a look of surprise. "That's it?"

"Yes sir. Thanks for all the help."

"Hey, thanks for coming." He gestured across the patio to the back door—it was the place I was standing the first time I laid eyes on Micah. I couldn't help but remember the scene when I looked at the big stones that made up the patio. "You won't have any trouble finding Claire and Thomas in the house," he said. He tossed his head toward the left. "I'm going to head on home and get dinner in the oven. Just leave the board and sawhorses where they are. I'll pick them up tomorrow." He put his hand on my shoulder again. "Thanks again for coming, Carly. It was good seeing you."

"It was good seeing you too," I said.

Claire happened to be standing in the kitchen when I came in through the back door. She didn't realize I'd be coming in that way, and she shot me a look of surprise but reached out to hug me the instant she realized who I was.

"Well hey Carly!" She held me at arm's length. "You look so beautiful!"

I'd gone home straight after work, taken a shower, and put on a fresh application of makeup just in case.

"Thank you," I said. "You do too." It was the truth. She was well put together every time I saw her.

"Thomas is *so* excited," she said.

"That's what Mr. Bennett said. I'm glad he's looking forward to it."

"Do you need help with your things?"

"Mr. Bennett helped me already. I'm all set up outside."

"Jesse, please. And call me Claire. You don't have to work outside. There's plenty of space in the arts and crafts room."

I shook my head. "Thanks, but we can't today. This one makes a mess. It's definitely an outside experiment." I glanced at her with a curious expression. "How many students do we have?"

"There are ten at art class, but a couple of them weren't sure if they could stay. Would you like to walk back there and see what they're doing?" She glanced at the clock. "They should be wrapping it up."

I nodded. "Sure."

I followed her down the hallway toward the art room. The house was familiar but entirely different at the same time. The living room was furnished with comfortable leather couches, and there was a huge entertainment system with a big screen TV and videogames. Built-in bookshelves were covered with books and all sorts of games. It was a fun, welcoming environment, one totally suited for a name like Happy House.

"This is really beautiful," I whispered as we made our way down the hall.

She looked back at me with a smile. "Thank you so much. We love it! I can't be here all the time so we have a lady from our church running it. She's great. Her name is Joan McClellan."

"I know Ms. Joan," I said.

"You do?"

"I think so... if it's the same lady who was painting with me that day."

Claire gave me a big smile and nod. "I'm sure it was. I believe Joan was here that day."

We came to stand in the door of the art room. Seeing the familiar gray color on the walls made me smile internally. The site of Thomas when he looked up and saw me made me smile for real.

"Carlyyyyyy!" he called, standing up and heading my way immediately.

The room was full of people. The students were sitting at tables that were arranged in a U-shaped formation, and the person I assumed was the art teacher was standing in the middle. There were people standing around the perimeter of the room. I figured they were the friends and loved ones of the students. Everyone looked my way as Thomas shouted my name and begin walking toward me. I smiled and held my arms out to hug him.

"Everyone, this is Ms. Carly," Claire said as Thomas hugged me tightly. "She's the one who came to do a science experiment with you guys."

"I know about science!" someone shouted.

"Hi Ms. Carly!" two others shouted.

"I'm staying for the science class!" someone said.

"Me too!"

"Me too!"

"Why don't you guys finish up what you're doing here, and Carly will be ready for you when you're done," Claire said.

"We're done," the art teacher said smiling. "We were just packing up our things."

All of the students stood and began taking off their smocks and packing up their brushes, and their caretakers moved forward to help them.

"Come see what I painted," Thomas said, dragging me to the area where he'd been sitting.

I looked at his mom for permission, and she smiled and gave me a little nod, so I followed him. He retrieved his picture from the table and handed it to me.

"I painted a treasure chest!"

"We *all* painted a treasure chest," his neighbor said, turning to face us. He had an ornery expression on his face, which made me want to take up for Thomas, even though I knew better since he had disabilities too. Thomas ignored him and looked at me with a smile.

"The Bible says to store up for yourself treasures in heaven where no one can steal them, and I'm gonna have lots of treasure in heaven."

"I'm gonna have pirate treasure in heaven," his neighbor said. "And I'm gonna have it on earth when I go to the beach next summer. My mom said Galveston has treasure."

"I'm not talking about Galveston anyway, Benji," Thomas said, rolling his eyes a little. I had to bite my lip to keep from smiling. I enjoyed seeing Thomas taking up for himself. "I'm not talking about pirate treasure either. In heaven there's other treasures. Like in heaven I'll probably look like my brother Micah and sing and play guitar."

The mention of his brother hit me for a second, but only until I realized that Thomas was saying he would be "normal" in heaven. That statement had an even greater impact on me then hearing Micah's name.

"And I'm gonna have my own mansion," Thomas added, staring at Benji daring him to say something back. "And I'm finally gonna get to see Jesu—"

Thomas stopped short of saying the name Jesus and I watched as he sank his face into his hand, pinching his nose and making a scrunched up expression. Then, all of a sudden, that high-pitched wheezing sound started.

"He's crying about Jesus again," Benji said in a frustrated tone to the art teacher as if he was tattling on Thomas.

"Thomas loves Jesus," she said patiently.

"Yes I do," Thomas said. "He's the one who died for me so I can go to heaven." He blinked extremely hard a few times and I could tell he was struggling to hold back another crying fit. "That's why you should love him too, because He died for you too."

I was touched by how emotional Thomas was. The amazing part was that it wasn't the thought of being normal in heaven that made him cry, it was simply the thought of seeing Jesus. There was peace and beauty in the simplicity of it, and I couldn't take my eyes off of Thomas. I didn't know much about

Jesus, but my heart told me Thomas was onto something.

Benji just shook his head as if he didn't understand where Thomas was coming from. "So when are we doing science?" he said in a matter of fact tone. He looked across the room. "Can I go to science class?" he asked the lady I assumed was his mom.

She nodded.

"How many do we have staying for science class?" the art teacher asked, loud enough to cut through the chatter. All of the students raised their hands.

I put a hand on Thomas' back. " I'm all set up in the backyard so I'll meet you guys out there." I motioned to his painting. "I love your treasure chest by the way. I think it's beautiful that you're storing treasures in Heaven." He handed it to me. "You can have it if you want."

He was so sweet that I had to struggle not to cry. I smiled and took it from him saying I'd be proud to own it, and would probably frame it for my new house.

I went outside to wait for them, and Claire promised she would walk everyone out to me as soon as they finished up. There were 10 students watching the experiment, and I instructed them all to stand in a line several feet away from my set-up where they could see what was going on.

Everyone else, including Claire, stood behind them to watch, seeming just as curious as the students.

"Okay, guys this is a super fun experiment because we get to watch things bubble up and explode."

"Like a bomb?" one of them asked, laughing.

"Not quite like a bomb. It's safer than that, but it's still fun. Have any of you ever seen the Mentos and Coke experiment before?"

All of them looked around to see if anyone would raise her hand, but no one did.

"Okay good. You're in for a treat. I want everybody to pay attention because the soda you see in front of you is going to bubble up and fly out of the bottle as soon as I add this candy to it."

I got ooh's and ahh's as a reaction from the students, which made me smile.

"So scientifically, it's a physical reaction that's happening. You know how when you take a sip of soda you can feel it bubbling in your mouth?"

Some of them looked confused, but most of them nodded and agreed.

"Well that's called carbonation. And carbonation reacts to the type of candy I'll be dropping into the soda. This certain type of candy makes it produce more and more bubbles really fast and all of a sudden, it will spray out of the container."

They murmured and looked at each other excitedly.

"Now I've done this experiment lots of times, so I already know what's going to happen."

I went behind the makeshift table and grabbed hold of one of the bottles. "I'm going to drop five pieces of candy into each bottle. Some of them will spray up this high." I demonstrated with my hand about 5 inches above the bottle. "And some of them will spray up this high." I stood on my toes and stretched my hand as high as I could to show a height of about 4 feet above the bottle."

They clapped at the potential of it going that high.

"Now, it's your job to guess which one will be the highest."

I came out from behind the table and gave them each a pair of safety goggles even though they wouldn't really need them from their place several feet away. I gave them each a handout with pre-drawn bottles and a pencil to record our results.

"We have Coke, Pepsi, Sprite, root beer, Coke Zero, and orange soda. You'll see six bottles on your piece of paper. Each of them is marked with a different type of soda." I glanced at the crowd behind the students. "Parents, they might need a little assistance keeping their data straight if you don't mind."

I shifted my attention back to the students. "You can draw your results above the little bottles, or you can simply write down how high you think it was or which one was the highest. There are no rules with how to chart your results. I just wanted you to have a piece of paper so you can keep track if you want to."

"When's it gonna explode?" one of the girls said, staring at the bottles with wide-eyed timidity.

I smiled. "As soon as I add the candy, but you'll be fine, I promise."

Chapter 9

The key was to add all five candies as quickly as possible. I had a little tube shaped contraption that helped me add them all at once. I explained to them what I was doing as I loaded the tube with candy. Aside from a little traffic noise and a barking dog in the distance, you could have heard a pin drop. They watched intently as I stood poised to drop the candies into the first bottle.

"You'll notice that I emptied out some of the liquid already," I said, pointing with my free hand to the two-liter. "I emptied the same amount out of each one, so they'll all have an even chance at winning the contest."

"What's the contest," Thomas blurted out, swaying front and back with excitement.

"Well, once we're done we'll see which one has the least liquid. If it has less liquid at the end, that means more of it came out during the experiment." I used my hand to demonstrate a gushing motion, which made them all laugh and clap. "All right, so I want you to get it in your head which one you think will be the winner. You don't have to say it out loud, but I want you to think about which one will have the highest geyser."

"What's a geyser?" one of them said, raising her hand.

"It's the shape the soda takes when it spews out of the top of the bottle. It looks like water coming out of a hose. So think about which one you think will have the biggest geyser—that'll be the winner. You can write it down on your paper if you want."

I watched as they made their decisions and some of them wrote something on their paper. I gave them about 30 seconds to finish up.

"Okay, are we ready?" I asked. I couldn't help but smile at all of their reactions. Some of them stared at me with untrusting expressions, and others couldn't stand still from all the excitement.

I did the Coke first. I dropped the candy into the bottle and stepped back as the geyser erupted from the top. The students watched in awe as soda shot into the air, and then seconds later settled down. They clapped, and cheered, and nudged each other before recording the results on their paper.

I knew Coke had a middle-of-the-road reaction. That's why I did that one first. Next came root beer, which was always a bit of a disappointment. The geyser only went a few inches above the bottle and not very much soda was lost. I heard one of the parents commenting that root beer was their pick and they were surprised it performed so poorly.

One by one, I went down the line, adding candy to the bottles and watching the reaction of the soda. I always had fun watching students observe this experiment, and tonight was even better than usual. Thomas and his friends were all so expressive and sweet. It was an absolute pleasure to be there, and I smiled the entire time.

Coke, Pepsi, and Sprite all had average reactions. Root beer and orange soda were both fairly disappointing, but I saved the best for last with Coke Zero. I did this experiment when I was student teaching, and one of the students said, "Coke Zero's the hero." It was a true statement that stuck with me. It always went the highest.

I saved Coke Zero for the grand finale. I dropped the candy into the bottle and we all watched in amazement as the Coke spewed what must have been ten feet into the air. It went so high that everyone gasped and took a step back even though they were standing far enough away to be out of danger. The reaction only lasted a few seconds, and once it settled down, everyone whooped and cheered.

I just stood there and watched their reactions for the next few seconds before calling them up to inspect the bottles so we could talk about how much liquid was left in each one. They gathered around and we talked for a while about our observations and scientific experiments in general. I gave them very basic information about making scientific observations, developing a hypothesis, and carrying out experiments. I was done about thirty minutes after I started, and afterward, the students and their caregivers all thanked me before making their way back into the house or to their cars.

I thanked them all for having me and told them what a pleasure it had been. Claire and Thomas volunteered to help me clean up, but I told them I would make quick work of it and they should go say goodbye to their guests.

It took me about 10 minutes to hose everything down and wrap it up, and by the time I made it inside there was only one other family there, and they were just leaving.

"That was so much fun, Carly," Claire said sincerely when I came inside. "Thank you for taking time out of your week to come do that." She gestured to the door. "Vanessa was just telling me how much she and Mark enjoyed it."

Thomas came to stand next to me. He stood close enough where our shoulders were touching and put his hand in mine, interlacing our fingers.

"You have some pretty cool friends, Thomas," I said. "I'm sure glad you let me come meet them today."

"Oh, you can come back tomorrow too," Thomas assured me, nodding his head as he stared at me seriously.

I smiled.

"She has a job, Thomas," Claire said. "It's a lot to ask for her to come do that for you guys—even once."

"You're not coming back?" he asked with real, true fear in his eyes.

"Of course I'll be back," I promised. I glanced at Claire. "Maybe we can set up something for a weekly or biweekly basis. Would that work for you?"

"That would be amazing!" she said.

Thomas continued to hold my hand, snuggling closer to me.

"I won't always need to be outside," I said.

"That'll be fine. You can just take over the art room if you want. Amanda's done in there at 5."

"Are we gonna do the Cokes again?" Thomas asked staring at me.

"Maybe sometime," I said, "but I have some other cool experiments for you guys to check out first."

He held my hand to his chest and gave me a huge smile. I returned it before looking at Claire. "Wednesday nights should be fine, but I'll get in touch with you about setting up a regular time."

"That sounds wonderful!" She reached out to hug me, and I hugged her back with one arm since Thomas still had a grip on me.

"I'm gonna go home and eat some dinner," I said, looking at Thomas. "I guess I'll see you next time. Thanks again for having me."

"You can eat dinner at our house," he said.

I smiled at Claire, hoping that hadn't made her feel uncomfortable. "Oh, thanks for the offer, but my little dog's waiting for me at home. If I took too long, he would wonder where I was."

"You have a dog?"

"I sure do. His name's Roscoe. He's a scruffy, brown mutt."

"Can he come next time?" Thomas asked, looking out of the corner of his eyes at his mom.

"Carly can bring her dog if she wants to," Claire said. "I'm sure everyone would love to meet Roscoe... as long as he doesn't bite or anything."

"He's really friendly."

Thomas pumped his fist before raising his hand above his head in the famous Thomas pose. "Yessss!" he said.

Claire turned off the overhead light, and we started making our way to the door. "Are you sure you can't come for dinner?" she asked.

She seemed sincere with the invitation, but I instantly shook my head in refusal. "Thanks so much for the offer, but I have to get home."

"Micah's coming to eat, isn't he, Mom?"

"As far as I know," she said.

We were walking when Thomas said that, and I seriously almost tripped. I had to concentrate on each step to keep from losing my balance. *Man, why hadn't I just agreed to go eat?* There was no way I could change my mind now, though. That would be totally obvious.

Thomas was still holding my hand as we walked out together. "Micah's my baby brother," he said, as his mom locked the door.

"He's not really a baby anymore, though, is he?" Claire asked, adjusting her purse.

"He's younger than me," Thomas reminded her.

"I met him," I said, smiling. "I think he was here the day when I came to help paint." I had to bite my own cheek to keep from laughing at myself for saying "I thought" he was there. *Who was I kidding?*

"He was?" Thomas asked with a doubtful expression.

"She probably did meet him," Claire agreed. "I'm sure he came up for the weekend to help."

"Is he coming over to eat tonight?" Thomas asked again, rubbing salt in an open wound.

"As far as I know, baby," she said, patiently.

I wanted desperately to ask the unaskable questions. *How's Micah? What's he look like now? What's he doing? And the most important question of all... Is he single?* I could never ask any of these questions, especially since I'd just acted like I wasn't even sure if I'd met him in the first place. What a dork.

"I guess you have to get home to your dog," Thomas said as we parted ways in the driveway.

"Yep," I said. "I'll tell him he gets to come up here sometime. He'll be excited."

"Maybe you can bring him to the fall festival too," Thomas said. "I think it's tomorrow."

I glanced at Claire, and she smiled at me. "You are welcome to come to the fall festival he's talking about. One of the members of our church has a big farm, and he has us out there every year. There's always a big turn out, and Roscoe's welcome to come too..." she smirked at Thomas. "But it's *not* tomorrow, silly. It's in a few weeks—the third Saturday of the month, whatever the date is."

"There's a corn maze, and a bonfire, and a hayride. Everybody plays football and capture the flag, and roasts weenies and marshmallows. And there's a hayride. Did I already say that?"

"That sounds like a lot of fun." I said.

"So you're coming?" he asked.

"Yeah, I'll come if you're sure it's okay."

"Oh sure, it's open to everybody," Claire said.

But it was overshadowed by Thomas throwing his hands in the air. "Yessss! Carly's coming with us to the fall-all-all festival!"

We hugged goodbye as we started toward our respective vehicles. "I'll see you before then, though," I promised. "I'll come back and do some more science with you next week."

"We're looking forward to it," Claire said, waving at me with her keys in her hand.

I was relatively sure that fall festival was the same weekend I'd be moving into my new place, but there was no way I was missing it, especially after botching the dinner invitation.

I knew better than to get my heart set on seeing Micah there, though, since a young, hot rockstar like him probably had better things to do than attend a church festival. I tried to tell myself I was going for

Thomas and I really didn't care whether or not I saw his brother, but that was untrue. I loved Thomas, and would be happy to go to the festival even if I knew for sure Micah wouldn't be there, but wow, what a bonus it would be if he was there. I didn't even care if he was married. I just wanted to see what he looked like—how he'd changed over the past five years.

Did I just have the thought that I didn't care if he was married? Of course I cared if he was married. It would be a super-wonderful day if I went to the festival, saw him, and he was not married, engaged, or otherwise taken. It would be the best day ever if he scooped me into his arms and we rode off into the sunset together. I could be married into this amazing family and live happily ever after with no more nightmares or scary crap happening to me. The end.

I was having all these thoughts as I dug for my keys and opened the door to my car, and I was smiling the whole time, well aware of how silly I was being.

"Bye Carly!" Thomas yelled, drawing me from my daydream. "I'll see you soon!"

"Bye Thomas!" I yelled back.

"I love you!" he yelled.

There was absolutely no way I would leave him hanging, so without hesitation, I yelled, "I love you too!"

I drove off wondering what it would have been like if I would have accepted their dinner invitation.

Would we have eaten and then curled up on the couch together for a little television and dessert? Maybe Thomas would have told Micah all about the experiment we did and Micah would think I was really awesome for being a science teacher. Maybe he was still gorgeous and this time he was unattached, and he'd walk me out to my car and kiss me at the end of the glorious, fun-filled evening.

I had to laugh at myself yet again. I should have been a writer with this kind of imagination.

Chapter 10

I thought about Micah quite a bit that night after the Bennetts invited me to dinner and I refused, but just as they'd done five years before, thoughts of him faded from my mind as the days went on. They faded even more quickly this time because I was in a different place with my outlook on men and relationships.

Looking back, I could recognize and appreciate that Zeke wasn't my life's love—maybe we weren't even a great match, but losing a boyfriend that way made me skittish about moving forward. I really didn't have much interest in building another relationship right away. In the four years since it happened, I'd purposefully kept myself too busy to even think about it. I finished my degree and teaching certificate quickly, and worked retail the whole time I was in college. In the back of my mind, I always assumed I would marry and start a family one day, but I hadn't even slowed down enough to consider anyone.

Micah's temporary entry into my thoughts was the first time in a long time I'd even thought about a guy in that way. Just the idea of him awakened a giddy feeling that I hadn't even realized I'd been missing. It made me feel good—like maybe I was turning some sort of corner.

That giddy feeling started up again as I drove to the address the Bennetts gave me as the location for the fall festival.

I had no idea what to expect, so I was completely taken aback when I pulled onto the property to find a huge party. There was a gigantic farmhouse front and center with a barn and several other buildings on the property. Some of the land was wooded and some cleared. It was gorgeous, and exponentially bigger than I anticipated.

There was a whole area over to the left that was roped off as a parking lot. A man wearing a safety vest motioned for me to drive down the fourth row of cars. There must have been more than a hundred cars there already. It was a much bigger deal than I expected, and I got nervous and shaky all of a sudden.

I drove down the row he indicated and parked about twenty cars back. I sat in my car for a minute, considering whether or not I wanted to go through with it or just turn right around and leave. I figured since there were so many people there, my chances of seeing Micah were good, but I honestly wasn't prepared for such a big deal, and was almost too nervous to stay.

I wondered how the parking attendant would react to someone who left right away. *Would he stop me and ask if everything was all right, or could I just wave goodbye and drive off?* Funny that the opinion of the parking lot attendant was even a factor. I laughed at myself as I checked the mirror for lip-gloss on my teeth or any other embarrassing things.

I had on a pair of tight fitting jeans with a cranberry colored sweater and a few necklaces. My dark brown hair fell over my shoulders. It was usually quite a bit shorter, but that was because I normally wore it curly. Tonight, I took the time to style it straight, and it seemed much longer. I ran a hand through it, checking for tangles.

Just then, a huge SUV full of kids pulled up and parked in the spot next to mine. Their family got out and began walking toward the farmhouse, which prompted me to stop stalling and do the same.

Several other groups were walking up to the action at the same time as me, and I couldn't help but notice that they were all carrying pots or pans. Obviously, it was some sort of potluck and I was showing up empty handed. My nerves escalated.

I followed everyone to a huge pavilion on the far side of the main house. The majority of the crowd was gathered there, and I knew it was my best shot at finding the Bennetts. The pavilion was full of tables and was packed with people sitting around them and standing up talking.

I should've texted Claire Bennett from the parking lot to let her know I was coming, but I didn't think about it at the time. I settled for walking up looking like a lost lamb.

I stared into the crowd, searching every table for a familiar face. "Carlyyyy!" I heard. It was Thomas's voice yelling out to me like a beacon of hope. I smiled at the sight of him walking toward me with his hands in the air.

"Thomassss!" I said as he approached me. "I didn't know if I'd be able to find you in this crowd," I said, hugging him.

He pulled back and regarded me with an extremely serious expression. I had no idea what he was thinking. "You don't like it?" he asked, seeming concerned.

I smiled. "Oh, no, I like it. I just thought I was lost for a second." He patted my back. "You're not lost. You're right here."

I let out a relieved giggle. "Yes I am," I said.

He touched my hair. "What happened to your hair?"

"I straightened it," I said. "Do you like it?"

"Yeah, my mom and Emily straighten their hair too," he said. "I saw that hot thing they clamp on it." He flexed his hand demonstrating the use of a flatiron, which made me giggle.

He drug me over to the table where his parents were sitting with four other people I didn't recognize. They greeted me and told me how happy they were that I could make it before instructing Thomas to bring me to the food area so I could make myself a plate. I started to refuse, but Thomas took me by the hand and began dragging me away immediately.

There was an area at the center of the pavilion with several long buffet tables. Every inch of them was covered with food. I didn't even know where to begin. There were at least thirty different types of soups and chilis in slow cookers and a ton of casseroles. Thomas and I stood in line, and I chose a few options that I hoped wouldn't end in a mess. I was holding a plate, but Thomas made sure I got a bowl of the tortilla soup their family brought, so my hands ended up completely full.

As if that wasn't enough, he insisted I go to the dessert table. There was a group of girls that looked to be my age standing around it when we approached.

"Who's your friend?" one of them asked Thomas.

He put his arm around my shoulders, almost making me spill the food I was balancing. "This is my best friend, Carly," he said.

The girl who asked smiled so brightly that, for some reason, it seemed fake. Then she stuck out her bottom lip a little, making a pouty face. "I thought *I* was your best friend," she said. She was obviously the ringleader. The other two just watched her, waiting to see what she'd say next.

Thomas got a little shifty at the thought of making her sad. "Carly comes to the Happy House and teaches science class," he said.

"Well, maybe I should come over there and hang out with you guys sometime," she said, with that same sugary sweet smile. "I've been meaning to do that."

The other girls nodded their agreement.

"I'm Gina," she said, holding her hand out for me to shake. This was impossible since I had a bowl in one hand and a plate in the other. I awkwardly extended my elbow in her direction and she scoffed for a split-second before pasting on that huge smile again.

"Carly," I said.

"How do you know the Bennetts?" she asked, shamelessly sizing me up.

I'd gone through high school and college. I knew a mean girl when I saw one; I was just surprised to find one at a church function—especially since she was the first new person I met.

"I volunteer at the Happy House," I said, answering her question. I wanted to add that Thomas had already mentioned that, but I decided to give her the benefit of the doubt and keep it friendly.

"My sister said you want to kiss Micah," I heard Thomas say.

I was stunned at his words and thought for a terrible second he was talking to me, but my head whipped around to see that he was staring straight at Gina."

"Me?" she asked, nervously putting a hand to her chest.

The girls standing next to her giggled and put their hands over their mouths simultaneously like twins.

"Emily said that?" Gina asked looking shocked and appalled. Her cheeks began to turn red and she seemed a little angry.

I figured she might say something rude to Thomas so I said, "She was probably mistaken. Come on Thomas, show me where we should sit to eat."

I turned and started walking off, and Thomas followed, but that didn't stop him from saying, (at full volume) "No she said Gina loves my brother and wanted to kiss him real bad."

"Okay, help me find your parents' table," I whispered, walking away as quickly as my feet could take me.

I couldn't help but smile at the thought of Gina's face turning bright red. I had to love Thomas. I thought about how she was sizing me up and wondered if her crush on Micah had anything to do with that. I was sure it did.

"So does your brother live in San Antonio now?" I asked as we headed to the table, but were out of earshot of Gina. I figured it was a good time to ask since Micah had just been brought up.

"He lives 1.7 miles from me," Thomas said. "He used to live 82 miles from me, but he moved home after his car wreck."

"Your brother got in a car wreck?" I asked, slowing to a stop in between two random tables.

Thomas nodded, but looked a bit distracted.

"Was he okay?" I asked, not ready to drop it.

"I have some scars, but I survived. Who's asking?" Thomas' face broke into a huge grin and he raised his hands above his head, nearly knocking the soup out of my hand. Maybe it was my nerves that almost made me drop the soup, but either way, it almost fell.

"Micahhh!" Thomas said. He looked at me. "Here's my baby brother right here," he said pointing at the guy who had spoken.

He was sitting at a table that was not anywhere near Claire and Jesse Bennett. I couldn't believe I had asked about him and we were standing only inches away. I instantly glanced around his table to find that he was sitting with a bunch of young people—probably my age or even younger.

I watched as Micah turned to face me. My heart was beating incredibly fast and seconds felt like hours as he faced me and begin taking me in.

Why was I standing their holding a bunch of food like a big dork?

He had changed. He seemed bigger—more masculine. A lot happens to a guy between 19 and 24. They go from being a boy to a man during that time, and the person I saw staring at me was definitely a man. He had the same gorgeous features, but he had filled out. I barely recognized him. His hair was still shaggy, but I could clearly see a scar on the right side of his face that went from his forehead, over the end of his eyebrow, and onto his cheek. It was undeniably handsome on him. I stared at it for a second, wondering if that was from the car accident before letting my eyes meet his. Those piercing green eyes had me feeling weak and shaky.

He was still in his seat, but he turned more fully and stared at me intently. "You look familiar," he said, with the hint of a smile.

Thomas put his hand around my shoulder again, causing my plate to jostle. "This is my best friend, Carly."

Micah smiled and nodded as recognition set in. "Oh, you're the girl who's been teaching science classes at the house, aren't you?"

I nodded.

"I'd stand up to shake your hand, but I can see they're full," he said, gesturing to my plate and bowl. I couldn't believe I was standing here holding a ton of food. What an oinker.

"Thomas tells me all about his science teacher," he said. "I know they really appreciate what you're doing over there."

"I love doing it!" I said smiling. It was the truth. I'd done a total of three classes so far and it was so much fun, I almost felt guilty every time someone made it seemed like I was doing a good deed.

"I'll let you get to your dinner, but it was nice meeting you," he said with a huge smile.

107

Did he think he was meeting me for the first time? Was I that forgettable?

"I met you a long time ago, but it was nice seeing you again," I said. I smiled and casually started to turn and walk away as if not expecting him to comment on my comment.

"Wait," he said. "We met before?"

I looked down at him again with a smile and nod, and he studied my face. "I thought you looked familiar! Where'd we meet?"

"At the Happy House a long time ago before it opened. You played a show opening for The Miffs that night, and I saw you there too."

A huge smile spread across his perfectly chiseled face. "Oh yeah! You're that same Carly? I had no idea! That's crazy! I didn't even recognize you!"

"You opened for The Miffs?" someone at his table chimed in, and Micah looked that way as they all started joking and laughing.

I already felt awkward enough standing their holding all that food, so I smiled as I turned to walk away again.

"Hey Carly," he said.

I turned to regard him from over my shoulder.

"I'll be over there in a few minutes."

I nodded and smiled as if it was no concern to me.

I was not hungry at all. I managed to pick at my food, but that was only because everyone else at the table had already eaten, and I knew they would notice if I didn't eat at all.

The pavilion was full of round tables, each of them seating six to eight people. We could easily see most of the property from our vantage point, and everyone sitting around my table explained what everything was.

There was a corn maze, a petting zoo, a huge bonfire, a gigantic slide that you ride while sitting on a burlap sack, several different games and challenges (including one where you toss corn cobs into a huge bucket), a hay ride, a "mystery" trail, (which I assumed was the Christian version of a haunted trail) pumpkin painting, face painting, and just about anything else you could think of. The pavilion was full of people and so were all of the activities. As I looked out, I wondered how big their church must be to host something this size.

"You guys didn't tell me Thomas' science teacher was the same Carly that I met during that work day," Micah said.

I didn't see him say it because he was behind me. My heart sank when I heard him say my name, but that was nothing compared to the way my stomach flipped when he put his hands on my shoulders. He gave them a little squeeze, and it was all I could do to keep my eyes open and remain composed.

I swiveled in my chair to stare straight up at him, "Yep, same Carly," I said as unaffected as I could.

He was standing so close that my ear was pressed right up against his stomach. It wasn't even funny how attracted I was to this guy. Unbelievable. He stared down at me. "You've grown up," he said with a slight grin.

That did it. I literally choked. I must have swallowed some spit down the wrong pipe because I began coughing uncontrollably. I turned away from him and leaned forward in my chair to finish my coughing fit. Thomas was sitting next to me and he patted me on the back.

"You okay?" Micah asked, once I was done.

"Yep," I said without looking up at him.

"If you're done eating, I'll walk you over to the cider mill to get a drink."

Chapter 11

I glanced back at Micah, who had just offered to walk with me to the cider mill, whatever that was. Logic would suggest that it was the place where they made cider. He was still standing behind me, and I regarded him from over my shoulder with eyes that were still watering from my coughing fit.

"Unless you're still eating," he said, pointing to my barely touched dinner.

"I'm done," I said. "I'll walk to the cider mill. I wanted to check out that corn cob toss anyway."

A smile spread across Micah's face. "Are you challenging me?" he asked, eyebrows raised slightly. He was goading me, and I loved it. I had been known to hold my own when it came to a tossing game, and I imagined the surprise on his face when I effortlessly roped the bucket.

"I'll go to the cider mill," Thomas said, drawing me from my thoughts.

Micah shifted his hand from my shoulder to his brother's. "Let me take her. I'm gonna talk to her about what she's doing for your next science class, and you can't hear that."

I glanced at Thomas, who was giving serious consideration to what Micah said.

"Why don't you let Micah and Carly catch up for a minute," Claire interjected. "You get to see her all the time."

Thomas conceded but didn't look like he was too happy about it. As I was standing, Claire shoved her half eaten chocolate cake in front of him, and his scowl turned to a smile. Claire winked at me just before Micah and I walked off.

He was considerably larger than the guy I remembered. I fell into stride next to him, wondering how much he had grown in the last five years, or if maybe he'd just filled out and seemed taller. I had on flats, but he was at least a head taller than me, and broad chested too. He was dressed casually but his taste was still impeccable. He had on fitted jeans and boots with a flannel shirt layered over a grey long sleeve thermal undershirt. His shaggy hair was darker than I remembered. It was loosely styled away from his face, but some of it had fallen over his eyebrow—his beautifully scared eyebrow.

"I guess you better tell me what you're next science lesson's about to keep me from lying to my brother," he said.

I smiled at him as we walked. "I think we're gonna watch a few items either float or sink on different liquids to demonstrate density."

"What liquids?"

I wondered if he was actually curious or if he was just making conversation. "Syrup, oil, and water."

He regarded me as if wondering what we could possibly do with that so I continued, "We'll put them all in the same container and they'll separate, one floating on top of the other in layers. Then, one by one I'll add items to the mix—a rock, a grape, a cork, and a piece of ice. They'll either sink or float depending on their density."

"That sounds pretty cool," he said. "I might have to come watch."

"You're welcome to."

We walked a few paces in silence. I could see the sign for the cider mill up ahead.

"Mom told me the class is a big hit. She said you brought your dog last time and everyone loved that too."

I smiled. "Roscoe's a trip."

"Roscoe, eh? What kind of dog is he?"

"He's a mutt. Some sort of wiry-haired terrier mix, I think. I have a picture if you want to see."

"I'd love to," he said.

I hadn't wanted to bring my purse when I got out of the car, so my phone was in one of my back pockets and a little cash was in the other. I fished around in there and pulled out my phone.

"I just moved into a new place this morning, and my roommate, Trish, just texted me a picture of her and Roscoe to convince me he was fine and that I should relax and have fun. She said she's in love with him."

I clicked on the picture and held my phone out for him to inspect.

"Roscoe must be quite the charmer," he said.

"He's awesome," I said. "I think it comes with being a mutt. Seems like everybody's got a soft spot for them."

He was staring at the picture and about to ask me something when Gina rushed to his side. Her sudden approach startled us both. "Heyyy!" she said, smiling brightly up at him. "Where are you going?"

"I'm taking Carly to get some cider," he said.

Gina linked arms with him and started walking with us. My blood pressure instantly started rising. Micah had been holding my phone, but he handed it back to me. "He's cute," he said.

I was annoyed, therefore I didn't respond.

"Please tell me you brought your guitar!" she said tugging at his arm. "A bonfire wouldn't be the same without some Micah music." Her pleading voice was meant to sound appealing, but to my ears, it sounded whiney. She was beautiful and probably really popular with everyone at the festival. I really didn't want to hate her, but it was hard.

"I brought it," Micah said. "I'll meet you guys over there in a little bit."

We were walking side-by-side, so I wasn't looking at them, but I could tell by his tone that he was asking her nicely to leave us alone. I wondered if she'd take the hint.

"Don't forget we're all gonna go scare the youth group on a hayride once the sun goes down," she said.

"I won't," he said, "I'll meet y'all over there."

"All right, I'll see you in a minute," she said, running off.

I glanced back to make sure she was gone. "Your girlfriend?" I asked.

"Who Gina? No, she's a friend—I'm sorry I should have introduced you. I forgot you don't know any of these people."

"I met her when I was getting my food," I said. "Thomas said she wanted to kiss you."

Micah busted out laughing. We were approaching the small, rustic building labeled Cider Mill when I said that, and Micah stopped walking and looked at me. "Thomas said that?" he asked, grinning.

I nodded.

"To her face?"

I nodded again. "And she didn't necessarily deny it," I said, shrugging and smiling, "so it seems you have a willing participant if you're ever in the mood."

"It might be a while," he said, his grin shifted and was now tinged with regret.

"Why's that?" I asked. "Not that I'm urging you to change your mind or anything—at least not where she's concerned."

There was a twinkle in his eye for a split second as he wondered what I meant by that exactly, but that sad smile made its way back to his face. He gestured to the scar on his face. "This isn't the only scar I had from that accident."

My eyes instantly scanned his body, which was completely covered with clothes. "There's a big one on my leg, and another one on my arm too, but physical scars aren't what I'm referring to."

"Oh," I said, understanding. I didn't know what else to say. I didn't want to prod him if he wasn't comfortable continuing.

He slowly walked to an out of the way spot on the side of the cider mill as if he wasn't quite ready to go in yet, and I followed him. I was just about to change the subject when he began speaking again. His face was solemn, and I knew that he was deeply affected by whatever was about to come out of his mouth.

"I was driving and my girlfriend was in the passenger's seat," he said. "We were going through an intersection at fifty miles an hour when we got hit." He leaned against the cider mill and regarded me with that same melancholy smile. "She was killed in that accident."

The air left my lungs in a sympathetic sigh and I put my face in my hand. "I'm really sorry," I whispered.

He pulled my hand down gently, making me glance at him. "I didn't mean to make you feel bad," he said, with a slightly bigger smile. "I just figured I'd tell you since you'd probably hear about it anyway. It was sort of a pivotal point in my life. It brought about a lot of changes."

"I guess so," I said. "Is that what made you move back to San Antonio?"

He nodded. "I lived in Austin after I graduated college. I had a good job there, and it was close enough that I visited regularly." He stared off into space for a few seconds even though I was standing right in front of him. "Anyway, I reevaluated after that and ended up coming home."

"Was it that girl I met at the bar that night?"

I asked. I could tell the question took him by surprise because he flinched slightly but answered without hesitation. "No, It wasn't her," he said, shaking his head. "We'd broken up by then."

I watched as he went inward for a few painful seconds.

"Her name was Natalie."

"I'm really sorry," I repeated.

"It's okay," he assured me. "It's been over a year since it happened, and I know time will continue to heal. It's just hard to get a scene like that out of your head, especially at first." He smiled and shrugged as if feeling bad to have burdened me.

I put my hand on his arm and looked into his eyes, searching them and letting him search mine. "I'm not just making stuff up when I tell you I know your pain," I said. "I don't know what you saw in that car accident, but you should know that I've seen something I desperately wish I could unsee."

Tears sprang to my eyes at the thought of finding Zeke. "It's been four years for me, and it does get better, but please just understand that I know where you're coming from." I glanced down and let out a tiny, humorless laugh. "And if it makes you feel any better, I didn't really feel in the mood to kiss anyone either."

"Did you get into a car accident too?" he asked.

My eyes met his again and I shook my head. I took a few seconds to debate how much I should tell him.

"What did you see?" he pressed, seeming genuinely concerned and interested.

"I found my boyfriend in his bedroom with a pistol—what was left of him, anyway."

He sunk his face into his hands and breathed out through his teeth. I was smiling sadly when he looked at me again. "Carly, I'm so sorry for you."

"It's okay," I said. "It's been four years, and like you said, it gets better with time."

I paused and he just stared at me, shaking his head. "I can't imagine," he said.

"Sure you can," I reminded him. We stared into each other's eyes for several long seconds, sharing a beautiful, unspoken empathy.

"How long did it take you to start dating again?" he asked.

I laughed nervously and began stammering. "What, me? Oh, I didn't really, I haven't really dated per say."

His mouth curved up in a genuine grin, which made color rise to my cheeks. "Please don't tell me it's been four years and you're still not able to move on," he said.

"It's only been a year for me, and my friends and family are trying to set me up with every available woman in Texas. I don't think I'll be able to hold them off much longer."

I smiled. "I could have moved on by now. I've just been really busy with school and everything."

"So you've kissed a guy since then, you just haven't been in a serious relationship," he said, as if stating a fact.

"I didn't say that, necessarily."

"Please don't tell me you haven't kissed a man in four years," he said staring at me.

"Okay, I won't tell you."

"But you have, right?"

"Why are you asking me that?" I said, smiling and shaking my head at him incredulously. I knew I was blushing; I could feel the heat in my cheeks.

"I'm asking you because I can't imagine you depriving yourself of a man's kiss for four years because of what your boyfriend did. It'd be a crime."

"I don't know if I'd call it a crime."

"It would be. You're a beautiful woman. Somebody's missing out."

I'd never been called a woman. Come to think of it, I wasn't sure if any guy had referred to me as beautiful before. Sure, my parents and grandparents had, but that didn't count. I found it hard to breathe regularly, and I had to sigh just to catch my breath. I stared up at him with a half-smile.

"Well you just said yourself that you didn't feel much like kissing Gina or anyone else for that matter."

His eyes roamed over my face, making me feel like my lungs weren't functioning at all. I could not get a good breath of air, and my stomach was tied in knots.

"I feel like kissing you right about now," he said.

He seemed completely serious when he said it, but I couldn't stop a nervous giggle. "Quit playing," I said, pushing at his broad chest.

He pinched my sweater and pulled on it a little, tugging me toward him. I stayed where I was standing, not taking his bait, and he took a small step closer to me.

"I think it's worth a shot," he said. "You know, just to see if we're still capable of doing it right. Like a science project."

I laughed. There was so much commotion going on around us. Children were laughing and playing tag, and people were walking by having conversations. I felt like I was in a dream.

"We don't do that kind of science in my class," I said.

"Then we'll call it something else."

"What?"

"At this point, you can think of it as doing me a favor," he said. He shrugged. "We can just pretend it never happened afterward if you want, but I think it'd be good for both of us to give it a try—just to see if we can still do it."

I could tell he was serious by the way he was staring at my lips.

This was definitely a dream.

I literally pinched my own leg as we stood there, and to my own astonishment I felt the pain of my thumbnail digging into my thigh.

"Well it's not really something we could just do right here in front of everybody, now is it?" I asked, still brushing it off like he was joking.

"Is that a yes?" he asked.

I glanced around before smiling up at him with a *you're impossible* expression. "I guess it's a yes, pending a spot where your whole church isn't staring right at us."

The next thing I knew, he grabbed me by the arm, and began dragging me toward the back of the cider mill.

Chapter 12

One second, I was standing next to an old, wooden building with Micah, and the next, I was being pulled around to the back of it. There were some trees and shrubs behind there, but we were still somewhat exposed—especially to people in the distance, near the entrance of the corn maze.

"I don't know what you think you're doing," I whispered as he marched me back there.

He stopped and turned to face me once we rounded the corner. The sounds of music, children playing, and people talking were barely audible over the pounding of my own heart. He stared down at me with a slight smile. Both of us were somewhat breathless.

"This is not private," I said, gesturing to the big open space behind me. "Someone can come back here any second."

"We better hurry then," he said.

I gave him a challenging glare. "Are you serious right now?"

"I'm quite serious," he said. "Do I still have permission?"

I smiled. "You're hilarious."

He cupped his hand around my jaw and patiently scanned my face. "You're beautiful."

I glanced down shyly. I should've just taken the compliment, but I got nervous and had to go and say something funny.

"It has been a long time," I said. "You're probably just desperate."

He ignored my comment, and instead just looked at me with a subtle smirk. He stared down at me for a long time, taking in every inch of my face. I had no idea what in the world he was thinking, so I started talking again when I should have probably just kept my mouth shut. "If we go through with this, I want you to know I'm okay with acting like it never happened."

He cocked his head at me and stared through narrowed eyes. "What do you mean *if* we go through with it?"

His hand was still on my cheek, and the warmth of it caused a shiver to run down my spine. I was out of my mind with nerves and anticipation. I took in the curve of his beautiful lips wondering what they would feel like when they touched mine.

"I'm gonna kiss you now, Carly."

He hesitated for a second, so I said, "Okay."

He stepped closer. I watched as he licked his lips before ducking to put them next to mine.

"It's been a long time," he whispered, his words creating little puffs of air against my mouth.

"I know," I whispered back.

I saw his chest rise and fall as he took a deep breath.

"We don't have to," I said, breathlessly.

"Stop trying to get out of it," he whispered with a grin. "I'm just taking it all in."

"You're gonna get us caught if you don't hurry," I whispered.

"You're gonna force me to take longer if you keep arguing."

I smiled and when I did, he put his lips on mine. It was torturously gentle. The only places we made contact were his hand on my cheek and his lips on mine, and both of them were barely there.

I closed my eyes and nudged forward ever so slightly. For a few glorious seconds, I enjoyed the feel of his lips on mine. It was at least as wonderful as I imagined. An ache formed deep in my gut and my blood turned to warm honey. I felt like I could melt.

Seconds later, Micah breathed in through his nose as he broke the contact.

I opened my eyes, assuming we were done. It was one tiny little kiss, and I felt weak and spent. I could see by the rise and fall of his chest that he was struggling to catch his breath too. I wondered if he felt the same sensations I felt.

"Yeah, that's not gonna be enough," he whispered.

"What do you mean?"

But before I could even finish the question, he put his lips on mine. It was a warm, flawless kiss that lasted only a split second before he pulled back again.

"I'm sorry," he whispered.

Another gentle kiss.

"Now that I've started."

Another one.

"I can't seem to stop."

And just then, just as I was utterly lost in the dream of having Micah Bennett's lips on mine, again and again, I heard my name being yelled.

"Carlyyyyy!" I knew it was Thomas, and the sound of it brought me crashing back to reality.

I looked at Micah with an astonished expression. "What are we gonna do?" I whispered frantically. I didn't give him time to answer. I put a hand on his chest, pushing him back a little. "You stay here for a minute. I'll go out there and meet Thomas, and you can come out in a minute so it won't be so obvious."

Without another word, I turned and headed down the side of the cider mill, running a hand through my hair and touching the corners of my lips to make sure everything was presentable.

There were lots of people in my line of vision, but I spotted Thomas instantly. "Hey Thomas," I said, walking toward him.

"I was looking for you guys in the cider mill," he said. "You weren't in there." His attention shifted to the area over my shoulder and he said, "Did she tell you about the science class?"

I turned around to find that Micah, despite what I told him, had not waited a minute to come out from behind the mill. I gave him a wide-eyed *you're in trouble* glance that only served to make him laugh.

"She told me about science class all right," he said to Thomas. "She showed me an experiment too."

"You did?" Thomas asked, beaming. "What'd you show him?"

I glanced back at Micah with an incredulous expression. "You're in trouble," I whispered, almost inaudibly, making him grin from ear to ear.

I turned to Thomas, who was just looking at me as if waiting for an answer. "I just showed him a trick I knew from a long time ago," I said.

"What trick?" he asked.

"Yeah, what trick?" Micah asked, amused.

I gritted my teeth wondering what in the world I could say without flat out lying. "The one where you rub two things together and it makes a spark," I said, to my own horror. I closed my eyes for a second, not wanting to glance at Micah who I knew would be thoroughly entertained.

"Really, can you show me?" Thomas asked.

I risked a horrified glance at Micah who was staring at me with wide-eyed amusement as if he couldn't wait to hear my response.

"I would," I said, shifting my attention to Thomas, "but I couldn't get it to work with your brother. It's been a long time since I've done that one. I'm going to have to brush up on my skills."

I spared a look at Micah. His amusement morphed to a look of challenge as I spoke. He opened his mouth to say something, but someone called his name.

"Micah, we need you over here!" someone said. We all turned toward the person who yelled to find a group of guys standing there looking like they were getting ready to play a game of football.

"We need one more!" one of them yelled.

Micah glanced at me and then at Thomas.

"Come on, dude, we got 5 on 5 if you play!"

"Do you guys care if I...?" he cut off when he saw me shaking my head as if it didn't affect me in the least.

"Are you coming?" the guy yelled.

"I'm coming!" Micah yelled back. "I won't be too long," he said, turning to me.

"I'm good," I said. "I've got my partner to show me around." I put my arm in Thomas' and he smiled at his brother proudly. Micah hesitated for a second but then smiled and ran off in the direction of the football game.

Thomas took me to the petting zoo where we got to feed goats, miniature donkeys, and llamas. I had seen enough of people get spit on by llamas that I squinted my eyes the whole time I was around them, just in case.

Afterward, we walked to the face painting area where Thomas and I both got a small pumpkin painted on our cheek. Several people came and introduced themselves to me, all of which were friendlier than Gina, who I noticed was with a small group of girls by the open field, watching the boys play football. I honestly didn't care. I was having more fun with Thomas than I would've been watching the football game and trying to look good every time Micah glanced at me.

Okay, in total honesty, part of me wanted to be over there watching the football game, but it was just the part of me that was still reeling from that unexpected kiss. Mostly, I was having a blast enjoying the festival with Thomas.

"I want to play the corn cob toss," I said, chewing a bite of caramel apple.

"I want to play the slide," Thomas said.

"How about we finish our apples, play one round of corn cob toss, and then we can slide at least five times after that?"

"That's a deal," he said, nodding.

We stood there, finishing our apples and watching the action around us.

"Where's Roscoe?" Thomas said, glancing at my feet with a worried expression as if he just noticed he was missing.

"He stayed at my house," I said. "He's with my new roommate, Trish."

"Is she gonna take care of him?" he asked with a mouth full of apple.

"Yep."

"Is she gonna let him outside to potty?"

"Yep."

"Is she gonna feed him?"

"Yep, she's a really good dog sitter."

"What's that mean?"

"It means she's really good at taking care of him. He's happy to stay there with her. She pets him a lot and loves on him like I do."

"That's what I do too," he said.

"I'll bet you'd be a good dog sitter too," I said.

"Yeah," he agreed, nodding.

A young couple came up to us just then. They were holding hands, but didn't have any children in tow. "Hey Thomas, who's your friend?"

"Oh, this is my best friend, and I'm a good dog sitter."

"You are?" the girl asked.

"Yep, because I know how to love on Roscoe just like Carly does."

"Is this Carly?" the guy asked.

"Yes," Thomas said.

They both smiled at me.

"And Roscoe's your dog?" the girl asked.

"He sure is," I said.

The guy held his hand out. "I'm Evan and this is my wife Lillian."

I shook his hand and then hers. "Carly Howard," I said.

"Do you go to our church?" she asked.

"No, I'm just friends with the Bennetts, and they told me this thing was open to anybody who wanted to come."

"Oh, totally," Lillian said, waving a hand in the air. "I've been going to church there for six years and I don't know half the people here."

"She's my science teacher too," Thomas said.

Lillian smiled at me curiously. "Really?"

I nodded. "I teach at Roosevelt full time, but here lately, I've been going to the Happy House once a week to teach a class.

"That's cool," she said with a huge smile. She came across as genuinely friendly, totally unlike Gina.

"We're going to play a tossing game and then we get to slide five times," Thomas informed them.

"Five times?" Lillian asked, looking amazed.

"Yeah, and Carly's gonna slide too."

"That sounds like a lot of fun!" she said.

"It was nice meeting you, Carly," Evan said.

I smiled and waved. "You too."

Lillian reached out to give me a hug. "If you ever decide to come to church make sure to come tell us hi," she said.

"I will," I promised. Evan and Lillian walked in one direction, and Thomas and I walked in the other. "I like your friends," I said.

"I have about a million friends."

I was sure he did. I agreed with him as we made our way toward the corncob toss. Not to brag, but I had some tossing skills that were formed way back in my recreation softball days. I wasn't great at many things but I was a boss at tossing a corncob into the bucket. I was sad Micah wasn't there to see it.

It was almost nightfall as Thomas and I rode the slide. It was our fifth trip down when I caught sight of Micah standing near the bottom. It was a double slide with several hills on the way down, and Thomas and I raced down each time. I was tempted to glance at Micah on my way down that last time, but I didn't. I watched Thomas like I'd been doing every other time.

I couldn't even find it within myself to glance at him once we were on the ground. I picked up the burlap sack and tossed it aside as I dusted off my jeans.

"I think Thomas won that one," I heard Micah yell.

"He won every time," I said, finally looking in his direction. It was growing dark, but there was enough light for me to see he was smiling. I smiled back.

Thomas came up next to me and put his arm in mine. I watched Micah watching us as we approached. His expression was unreadable, and I wondered what he was thinking.

"I like your pumpkin," he said.

He was staring straight at me, but Thomas said, "Thank you. Justine painted it."

"I'm glad you caught me," I said. "I was just about to leave."

The crowd had thinned out considerably. There were very few little kids running around, and I figured it must have been close to their bedtimes. There were still quite a few people, but most of them were teenagers and adults.

"You can't leave without sitting by the bonfire for a few minutes," he said. "It's tradition."

"I have to get back to Roscoe."

"Yeah, and I'm a great dog sitter," Thomas informed him.

"I was hoping you could stay for a little bit," Micah said. "I can't stop thinking about that experiment you showed me... the one that didn't work."

I shot him a warning glance, which only made him smile.

"Because the thing is... I thought it *did* work," he said, looking comically confused.

My warning glance intensified. "No," I said, shaking my head. "I'm pretty sure it didn't."

"Well, we have to try it again," he said in a matter of fact tone.

"You can come to my science class tomorrow," Thomas said.

"It's not tomorrow," I reminded him. "It's in four more days."

"You can come to that," Thomas said.

"I might have to," Micah said with a hint of challenge. He shrugged. "So are you staying?"

"Just for a few more minutes."

Chapter 13

Trish was there when I got home that evening.

It was Saturday, and our other roommates, Ryan and Isaac, were both out, but Trish stayed home to dog sit Roscoe. She thought about coming with me to the festival, but she was feeling lazy after a long week at work, and wanted to chill. That worked out better for Roscoe anyway, since he was still getting used to the new house.

Trish had just started dating a guy, and he'd come by earlier, but was no longer there when I got home from the festival at 9pm. She was watching a movie in the living room, and she paused it as I opened the door. Roscoe ran over to me with his tail going about a hundred miles an hour. I stooped to greet him in the high-pitched *that's my baby* tone I always used, and rubbed him behind the ears.

"He's been curled up on the couch with me since I started this movie," she said.

"Were you lovin' on your Aunt Trish?" I asked, still petting Roscoe.

I took off my shoes and purse and stashed them in their places by the door. "It must have gone well," she said.

I looked at her with a regretful expression. "I'm sorry I'm later than I thought I'd be. I ended up having fun, and the farm's about thirty minutes from here."

She shook her head. "Don't be sorry. We had fun. I was glad to have a movie partner." She patted the seat next to her and Roscoe jumped up beside her again as if demonstrating what an ideal movie partner he was.

I followed him to the couch and took a seat, sighing and letting my shoulders slump with relief. "So..." she said curiously. "How was it?"

I looked over at her without taking my head off of the back of the couch. "He kissed me," I said, unable to contain a smile.

Her brows furrowed. "Who?"

"Micah Bennett."

"Get out!" she said with a shocked expression, leaning forward to slap at my leg. "I thought you didn't even know if he was going to be there."

"I didn't."

"I thought you haven't seen him in five years."

"I hadn't."

"So how did he kiss you? Were you bobbing for apples and it just sort of happened by accident or something?"

I laughed, and then sighed and shook my head as I remembered the chain of events. "His girlfriend died," I said. "It happened about a year ago, and he was in the car with her."

She gasped, and covered her mouth with her hand. "That's terrible," she said.

"I know." I stared into space, thinking about the conversation I had with him. "He was hurt too, but he said the worst part was seeing her." I hesitated. "Anyway, I ended up telling him about what happened to me, and somehow we mentioned that neither of us had moved on since. One thing led to another and the next thing I knew, he said we should kiss each other, you know like for an experiment to see if we could still do it or whatever."

"What?" she asked, scrunching up her nose as if that was the weirdest, unromantic thing she'd ever heard.

"I'm not saying it right," I said. "I can't remember exactly how it happened, but we were standing there next to a building talking about it, and he came up with this bright idea that we'd kiss each other." I threw my hands in the air. "I'm totally not explaining it right. It was awesome. He was funny and gorgeous, and I'd do it again in a New York minute."

It must have been obvious how giddy I was, because she grinned at the sight of me. "He's still hot, I take it?"

I sighed dramatically and let my head hit the back of the couch again. "So hot," I said. "He has a scar on his eye from the accident and it only makes him hotter, if that's even possible. Plus, he's a lot bigger than the last time I saw him. I think he turned into a man."

"You're totally in loooove!" she said.

"If I could fall in love at first sight with anyone, it would be Michael Bennett. It's too bad I told him we should pretend like this never happened."

She slapped my leg again. "You did not!"

"I sort of did."

She hit me again, making me giggle.

"I think he mentioned it first, and it made me nervous, so I said it. I was a little out of my mind."

"Well, you better find a way to take it back."

"I might have also said that I didn't enjoy myself," I said.

"What? Why in the world would you say something like that?"

"I didn't say it in those words. It's a long story. We were referring to it as a science experiment, and when we talked about it in front of his brother and I sort of led Thomas to believe that the experiment didn't work. I didn't mean to say I didn't enjoy myself, but it might've come out that way."

Her expression was utterly dumbfounded, which made me laugh.

"It's too hard to explain," I said.

"Basically, you loved it, but you made him think you didn't."

"Maybe a little." I said cringing and scrunching my face up.

She laughed. "Who knows, it might actually work in your favor."

"He already mentioned trying again."

"Oh snap," she said, covering her mouth. "So was that it? You talked, you kissed, and you came home?" She gestured to my face. "There must have been face painting somewhere in there."

"Oh there was a ton of stuff. Micah went off to play flag football with some of his friends while Thomas and I hung out. There were tons of things to do. You really should come with me if I go next year." I glanced at her with a sideways smirk. "I didn't even tell you the best part."

"What?"

"They had this huge bonfire. There were like fifty people sitting around it once the sun went down, you know, roasting marshmallows and everything. Micah brought his guitar and sang for everybody."

"He just busted out into a song?" she asked.

"It sounds cheesy, but it was amazing. He's hilarious, and he started by playing and singing an impromptu song about fall. He talked about specific things and people at the festival, calling people out and making everyone crack up. It seemed like it was impromptu, but I have no idea how he could have made up something that good on the spot. I'd seen him play with his rock band a long time ago, and I knew he had a good stage presence, but I'd never seen him like this. He had everyone's undivided attention, and he never for a second seemed awkward or nervous. Everyone just laughed and clapped along like he was the best thing since sliced bread. It's amazing to watch someone with that much talent. He was like a hot Jack Black with the most perfect singing voice."

"You are soooo in love," she said.

"I am not," I said. "I just can't believe how talented he is. His talent's magical or something. I wish you could see him play and sing. You'd agree with me."

"Is he still playing in a band?"

"I was asking Thomas about it, and from what I gather, I think Micah's doing Christian stuff now."

"Really?" she asked wrinkling her nose again as if Christian music might be second rate.

I shrugged. "I don't know for sure," I said. "Thomas started bawling in the middle of telling me about it, so I didn't get the whole story."

"Why'd Thomas start crying?"

I shrugged. "He does that when he gets touched. It's usually when he talks about God."

"So they're big time Christians?"

"Yeah. I think so. I'm not sure about Micah, but Thomas is for sure."

"What do you think about that?" she asked.

I shrugged. "I don't know. I've been thinking about it some lately. Sometimes I'm drawn to the idea."

"I love God," she said, surprising me.

I raised an eyebrow at her. "You do?"

She laughed. "Thanks a lot. Is it that hard to believe?"

"No, I've just never heard you mention it."

She shrugged. "I'm probably not as good a Christian as I should be, but I did get saved when I was in high school, and I do believe Jesus is the way and everything."

I almost told her we should try the church the Bennett's went to, but I decided to save it for another day. I didn't say anything for a minute or so. I just put my hand on Roscoe's belly and stared at the ceiling as I contemplated everything.

"Are you gonna see him again?" she asked, breaking the silence.

"I'm sure I will; I just don't know when," I said, still staring upward.

I stayed out there for a few more minutes before telling her I was going to take a shower. She said she was going to stay in the living room to finish her movie, and I said I'd probably be back out for a snack. Roscoe came with me into my room even though she protested and begged him to stay.

I was thankful that he seemed content in our new house. I did too. It was a comfortable place, and judging from the state of the common area, my roommates were all neat freaks. It was the first night in my new room, and I slept like a baby. Perhaps it was that I felt at home there, or perhaps it was the memory of Micah's kiss. Either way, I was content and comfortable, and Roscoe was too.

The next day was Sunday, and it took me just about the whole day to get everything put in its place in my new room. My week at work was busy as usual, and my Wednesday evening science class snuck up on me. I was doing the experiment about density with oil, water, and syrup, and I smiled as I brought my supplies in the house, remembering how I explained it to Micah.

My smile faded the second I stepped foot in the door. Gina was standing in the living room talking to Claire Bennett. Both of them looked at me when I walked in. Claire was wearing her usual smile, but Gina didn't hesitate to look me over from head to toe as if she was sizing up the competition. That's how I took it at least. Maybe that was just the face she made all the time, but it sure felt like she had distaste for me. I wanted to scowl back at her, but I remembered Claire was looking at me, so I smiled and tried to seem genuinely happy to see them both.

"Hey Carly!" Claire said. "Do you need help?"

"No ma'am, I've got it."

She gestured to Gina. "Did you get the chance to meet Gina the other night at the fall festival?"

"Yes ma'am, we met," I said, not looking at Gina.

"Carly does a science class every Wednesday," Claire told Gina.

"She told me all about it," Gina said, with that syrupy sweet smile.

Was I the only one who could see through that thing? I had to tell myself to chill out and not let her presence bother me.

141

"Oh, I didn't realize you two got to know each other already," Claire said.

"Oh, we didn't really. She asked me how I knew Thomas, and I told her about doing the class. That was really all we said."

"Well, Gina decided to volunteer with us," Claire said as if that was exciting news.

It took great effort on my part not to let frustration show on my face. I was holding a canvas bag full of supplies in one hand and a big glass container in the other, and I gripped them both tightly as I squeezed out a forced smile. I was sure mine looked as fake to Gina has hers looked to me.

"Great," I said. "I'm gonna go ahead and get set up." I tilted my head toward the hall letting them know which direction I was headed before I glanced at Gina. "It was nice seeing you again."

"Likewise," she said.

I groaned inwardly and rolled my eyes when I had my back turned to them. Everything about this girl irked me. It even frustrated me that she said the word likewise. I never used that word, but I always liked it when I heard someone else say it, and I wanted to try it one day when I had the opportunity.

It didn't help that she was beautiful and extremely well put together. I cringed as I made my way down the hall toward the art room wondering if she'd be there every Wednesday.

All my resentment melted away the instant I saw my students—especially Thomas. They were excited to see me. I felt a sense of unconditional love when I was around them that made me happy right down to my bones. I wasn't sure if it was volunteering in general, or if it was these students specifically, but I loved it. I regretted that it took me so long to find this beautiful outlet in my life.

I helped them clean up the mess created by the art class before setting up my experiment and giving the students their handouts. I started off with a speech, giving them the basics of density and matter. A few of the students stared at me the entire time as if I wasn't making any sense, but I had learned to ignore it since that was the face they made week after week, and they always told me how much they enjoyed it afterward.

I was 15 minutes into the class and just starting the actual experiment, when a shadow darkened the doorway. I assumed it was Mrs. Bennett since it was a regular occurrence for her to peek in on my classes. I assumed Gina would be with her even though I hoped that wasn't the case and she'd already gone home.

I glanced at the door with a smile, and my heart leaped into my throat when I saw Micah Bennett standing there.

"My baby brother is here!" Thomas yelled. I looked at him to find his arms raised above his head as he beamed at Micah. I looked back in Micah's direction to find him smiling at Thomas with a finger over his mouth, telling him to keep it down.

"It's okay," I said. I looked at the class. "Does everybody know Thomas' baby brother?"

They murmured around the table, most of them nodding but some shaking their head.

"Well, this is Micah." I looked toward the door. "We were just about to do an experiment if you want to join us?"

Chapter 14

"I'd love to," Micah said without hesitation.

He entered the classroom and went straight for one of the extra chairs that lined the wall, only he didn't sit in it like I assumed he would. Instead, he picked it up and carried it to the table so he could sit with the students. He made Thomas scoot over and squeezed into the empty space between his brother and Benji.

Thomas was thrilled with the new addition to the class, and he put his arm around his brother, before turning to beam at everyone. I tried in vein to contain a smile as I passed Micah one of the handouts and a pencil.

One at a time, I poured the water, oil, and syrup into the glass container. Everyone reacted in amazement at the way they separated and formed visible layers.

Once the liquids settled completely, I dropped items into the container one by one. Before I added each one, I asked them what they thought would happen.

"Okay, so I have a rock," I said. I held the small stone up for their inspection before holding it above the glass container full of liquids. "What do you think the rock will do?" I asked.

No one answered right away, so I continued, "It might float on the top, or it might sink to the bottom. Do any of you have an idea?"

Several of the students yelled out what they thought the rock would do. I carefully dropped it, and we watched as it penetrated all three layers of liquid and sank to the very bottom.

Everyone cheered. "I heard some of you say you thought it would sink," I said. "If that was your guess, you were right. I want all of you to take a second to mark your handouts. You can just draw a rock on the bottom of the container you have on your paper. A rock's just a circle, so don't stress about getting it perfect."

I watched as Thomas marked his paper and then peeked onto Micah's paper to see how his brother was doing.

I then added an ice cube, a grape, and a cork to the container, pausing between each one so they could watch the results and mark their papers. The rock sank to the bottom of all the liquids, resting on the bottom of the glass container. The grape sank to the bottom of the oil and water but floated on the syrup. The ice cube sank to the bottom of the oil but floated on the water. And the cork floated on top of everything.

You could clearly see the layers of liquid and the items floating on each one, but I walked around with the container so everyone could see it more closely. I wasn't sure all of them quite grasped the concept of density, but they seemed to love the experiment, and couldn't get enough of looking into the container.

I asked if any of them had questions, and Benji raised his hand. "When are we gonna do the Coke spraying thing again?" he asked.

"You guys have already seen that," I said. "Do you really want to see it again?"

They started elbowing each other and murmuring excitedly. I got enough sounds of approval that I said, "Shhhh, okay I'll take a count and we'll see about doing that one again sometime. Show me by raising your hands. How many of you want to see the Coke and Mentos experiment again?"

Every single student's hand shot into the air faster than I could blink. Micah's hand was right there with them. I let out a little laugh. "Okay, it looks like we'll have to do that one again," I said. "Maybe I'll bring it next week."

Samantha raised her hand and I called on her. "I think Coke Zero will win," she said. They all started agreeing with her, so I cut in telling them I'd be bringing new challengers for Coke Zero next time.

I told them all goodbye and to have a great week, and they started packing up their things and heading for the door. I went to the adjoining bathroom where I fished the items out of the container and disposed of the liquids. By the time I turned to head for the classroom again, Micah was standing in the doorway, leaning casually on the frame.

I secretly hoped he'd be standing there, but I still acted surprised to see him. I smiled. "Did you finish your handout, Mr. Bennett?"

"That's Micah!" Thomas said, popping his head around the corner when he heard my formality.

I inched toward the door but stopped before I got too close. "Did you finish your paperwork, Micah?" I asked, smiling. He stared down at me with a totally unreadable but intent expression. His appraisal made me antsy. "Did you like it?" I asked, feeling the need to fill the empty space between us with words. He looked at me for several more seconds before the corner of his mouth turned up in a grin. It was an irresistible sight. He was dressed in fitted khakis and a button up shirt, looking every bit the male model. I was helpless to do anything but stare into his intense green eyes. "Did you enjoy the experiment?" I repeated.

"I've enjoyed every single experiment I've ever done with you." Thomas had been facing away from us, watching his friends leave, but he turned to chime in at Micah's words. "This is your first time to Carly's class," he said.

"Yeah, this is your first class," I said, looking at Micah with challenge as I walked past him.

"Let me take you to dinner," Micah whispered, reaching out to barely touch my arm as I passed.

I glanced at him with a curious expression.

"Carly can come to dinner at our house," Thomas said. Micah thought Thomas hadn't heard his whisper, but obviously he was wrong.

"I can't tonight," I said talking to mostly Thomas since I wasn't sure if Micah meant tonight or not. "I should really get back home to see Roscoe. I'm not sure if any of my roommates are home to let him out of his kennel."

"Why don't you call them?" Micah asked.

"Why didn't you bring Roscoe?" Thomas said.

I was overwhelmed. It was a dream come true for Micah to ask me to hang out with him, but I didn't want to seem to eager.

"He stayed home this time since I had my hands full with all my supplies," I said, looking at Thomas. I shifted my attention to Micah. "Were you referring to tonight?" I asked.

"Yes," he said. "I was thinking we'd leave from here."

"Are you coming to my house?" Thomas asked.

"Probably not this time, brother," Micah said, tenderly reaching out to mess with Thomas' hair. "I was hoping you'd let me take Carly out this one time since you get to see her more than I do."

Thomas looked a bit annoyed, but went back to packing up his things.

I got all of my supplies together and the three of us went into the living room to meet Claire. Gina was nowhere in sight, a fact for which I was grateful. One family was lagging behind everyone else, so they ended up walking out with us when Claire locked up.

"Did I tell you Gina's volunteering with us," she informed Micah as we made our way outside.

"Gina Young?" he asked, looking surprised.

"Yeah, she came in earlier to ask what she could do to help. She left just before you got here."

Claire obviously had no idea what sort of crush Gina or I had on her son or she would have never said something like that in front of me.

"What'll she be doing?" he asked.

Claire shrugged. "She's coming in for a couple hours a week—probably on Monday or Wednesday. I told her we always needed help with cleaning, and she said she'll just do whatever's needed."

"That's cool," Micah said.

Don't you dare begrudge them the help they need just because a girl rubs you the wrong way. That is so selfish. Volunteers are good. Smile. Just smile.

Micah was helping me out with my supplies or I would have probably turned tail and run home during that conversation.

"What are you doing for dinner?" Claire asked, thankfully changing the subject.

"I'll probably stop at that little Greek place," he said. "I'm trying to get Carly to let me buy her a sandwich."

"Oh!" she said. There was a lot implied by that one word. It was laced with such surprise that it was obvious that she never considered Micah wanting to take me somewhere. Or maybe that's just how I took it and it wasn't what she meant at all. I was probably just annoyed that she brought up Gina.

Micah and I told Claire and Thomas goodbye, and he walked me to my car. "So what do you think?" he asked, standing there while I stashed the supplies into the backseat of my two-door sedan. "Will you let me buy you dinner? I promise I won't make you do any scientific research with me."

His reference to scientific research was obviously code for kissing, and my gut clenched at his mention of it even though he was saying he *didn't* want it to happen. I went from sick with anticipation to sick with disappointment within a matter of seconds. *Just keep smiling.*

I sighed as I straightened to stand next to him. "I guess," I said. "As long as you promise not to make me work. I'm officially off the clock."

He held up his hands in surrender. "Just a bite to eat," he said. "You want to ride with me? It's not that far, and I can bring you back here to get your car afterward."

Micah had a nice truck. I rode in the passenger's seat, imagining that was my regular spot. I pictured us as a couple and thought about what it would be like to ride with him places all the time.

We talked about his job the whole way to the restaurant. He was in construction like his dad, but he'd gone out on his own and started a business

151

specializing in concrete. His expertise was with staining and finishes, and his business did mostly commercial jobs. He was really humble about the whole thing, but I could tell by the way he explained it that his company had really started to take off despite the fact that it was so new.

The restaurant was a tiny, casual place where you order at the register and they call you up to get your food once it's ready. Micah ordered a Gyro and I ordered a Greek salad, and we sat across from each other, looking down at the delicious food. I noticed that he closed his eyes for a second before he dug in. He didn't make a show of it, but I assumed he was praying.

"I meant to tell you, I really loved your Halloween song the other night," I said.

He had taken a bite, and he laughed as he chewed. Even his chewing was handsome. Muscles in his jaw and temple worked, and I had to stare at his shirt to keep from gawking at him.

"I'm serious," I said. "I can't believe what a good musician you are. Thomas was telling me you're playing with a Christian band now."

"I am."

"How'd that come about?" I asked.

"Are you asking how I met the guys or how I came about wanting to play Christian music?"

"Both, I guess."

"I met the guys at church, but I don't play with the same guys all the time. The band changes depending on who's available when I'm playing. I'm recording an album soon, though, and I have a core group for that. There's five others besides me."

"Do you mostly do songs you wrote?"

"Yeah. I love writing. I was writing all the stuff for Sweet East too."

"So what made you change to Christian music?" I asked.

He smiled as if he knew that question was coming. "It's funny how God can use the most unlikely thing to hit you," he said. "I grew up in the church, and if you would have asked me, I would have told you that Jesus Christ was my savior, but for a long time, it really didn't show it the way I was living. I was just doing life in college, and Jesus was pretty much on the back burner. Anyway, I had made a couple of albums with Sweet East, and they did pretty well on iTunes. We were doing gigs every weekend and drawing some good crowds, but it just felt like it wasn't enough. We had some success, but I just kept wanting more, more, more—feeling like nothing was enough."

He paused as if to gauge whether not I was still interested and I smiled and nodded.

"So one weekend when we weren't playing, I came home. Thomas and I were both sitting in the living room and mom asked me to read to him. She's always buying different kinds curriculum for him so he can learn new things, and she asked me to read out of a music appreciation book thinking it would appeal to both of us. The story happened to be about Johan Sebastian Bach. Do you know who he is?"

I nodded. "Of course."

"Did you know he was a Christian?" he asked.

I shook my head.

"Me neither," he said. "I had no idea until I read to Thomas that day. Apparently, he was a really devout Christian. He worshiped God through his music. His only goal in life was to please God and help others with his talent. It said he never even tried to become famous or make his works well known—that he didn't even try to preserve the things he wrote, he just wrote to please and worship God, and that was it."

"Wow," I sighed. "That's crazy."

"I know, right? He would write initials at the end of his compositions. They were S.D.G., and they stood for the Latin phrase Soli Deo Gloria, meaning to the glory of God alone."

Micah took the final bite of his gyro and we sat in silence for a minute. I found myself trying to remember some of Bach's famous work and imagined him with a quill or whatever he wrote with, composing it for God alone.

Micah used a napkin to wipe his mouth before crumpling it up and dropping it in the empty basket in front of him.

"Something clicked in me that day," he said shaking his head. "I'd been spending so much time and energy trying to make people notice and appreciate me as an artist... constantly wondering what other people thought of my music. Something about the idea of using my art to glorify God alone seemed right. I was liberated and humbled all at the same time. I mean, if someone like Bach was willing to use his talents for God alone, how much more willing should I be?" He paused and shrugged. "I know there's a stigma to Christian music or whatever, and honestly I don't care. I didn't find true happiness in using my talent until I wasn't trying to impress anyone but God with it."

Chapter 15

Something about Micah's story hit me like a ton of bricks. I didn't think I necessarily had a talent I could use as a form of worship, but the mindset appealed to my soul on a level I didn't quite understand. He seemed grounded and content, and I found myself wanting that same feeling.

"So you switched over to writing Christian music?" I asked.

"I still write love songs, and tons of random silliness, but yeah, I starting putting pen to paper with Bach's story in mind, and inspiration came easy. The more I do it, the easier it is, and the closer I feel to God. It's not like I changed my whole life and started being Mr. Perfect Christian all the time, but I do feel close to Him. I enjoy singing to Him and about Him, and I enjoy the opportunity to see my music help other people. Sometimes it makes me feel so good, I think it's more for me than it is for Him."

He paused, but I was chewing a bite of salad, so he continued.

"The girl you met at that bar broke up with me when the change took place." He shrugged. "I didn't think I changed at all, I mean, I still had the same sense of humor and everything, but she wasn't into my life being more Christ centered. I hadn't been going to church long when I met Natalie. I thought I was on the right track. I was open and willing to being used by God, and dating a good girl, and then, bam—out of nowhere the accident."

"Did it make you want to turn around and run the other way?" I asked.

"You'd think it would have, but it did the exact opposite. I can't imagine trying to go through something like that alone... and I'm not talking about family. I mean internally—some things can only be addressed supernaturally, you know? The guilt and the vision of her dying would have been too much to bear without leaning on God. Anyway, I did the opposite of turning away. I wrote prolifically during those first few months."

"Do you ever wonder why God would allow that to happen to you?" I asked.

He smiled. "All the time. But I wonder it in a happy, expectant way."

My face must have shown my confusion because he laughed. "What I mean is that I know for a fact in the deepest parts of my heart that God has a plan, and that specific pain is part of it. I find it easy to trust that."

"I wasn't raised going to church, and I've only recently been thinking about God," I admitted. "Sometimes I think if I'd been closer to Him during the past few years, everything with Zeke would have been easier."

Micah shook his head. "I honestly don't know how you did it without Him."

"I guess I pray to Him as good as I know how when I'm feeling scared or wake up from a nightmare, but I doubt I'm doing it right."

"There are no rules," he said. "God hears you when you talk to him, period. There's no protocol."

"What about for getting into heaven?" I asked.

"What about it?"

"What's the protocol for that?"

"It's not complicated," he said. "It's just a matter of knowing that your sins separate you from God and believing that Christ died and rose from the grave to bridge the gap between you and God. Once the significance of that sacrifice sinks in, then you feel sorry for your sins, and you ask Him to live in your heart. You just tell Him you desire to trust and follow Him."

"And that's it?" I asked. "You don't have to say certain words in a certain sequence like a magical prayer or something?"

He shook his head. "Not really. Churches usually lead people in a sinner's prayer, but it's basically what I told you just now. All that matters is that your heart understands and agrees with the things I just said."

"Say what a church would say," I said.

"What?" he asked, looking confused.

"That sinner's prayer you just mentioned. Say it."

He smiled. "You want me to recite it?" he asked with wide eyes.

"Yeah."

"I mean, I don't know how good of a job I'd do on the spot like this. I'm not a pastor or anything."

"Try it," I said.

He smiled and shook his head, but I could tell his wheels were turning as he attempted to put something together. He looked around to see if anyone was paying attention to us, and then he said, "I guess it would go something like, Jesus, I know I'm a sinner, and I ask your forgiveness. I believe You died for me and rose from the grave. I turn from my sin and invite you into my heart and life. I want to trust and follow you as my Lord and Savior."

He spoke softly but to the point as if he couldn't quite believe I was making him recite that in the middle of a Greek restaurant, but he smiled afterward as if surprised by how good it sounded. I smiled back at him and set down my fork. It had been a while since I took a bite, and I was no longer hungry anyway.

"So if in my heart I said what you just said, then that's it—that's all I have to do?"

"Did you?" His eyes popped open in a look of surprise that was so cute I couldn't help but giggle.

"Probably," I said, wiping at a few tears that were trying to escape the corner of my eyes.

"Did you seriously?" he asked putting his palms on the table and leaning toward me with wide eyes. "Just now?"

He was so animated and funny that I was laughing and crying at the same time.

"I think I did. I tried to. I wanted to."

He clapped his hands in front of him one time so loudly that it drew glances from several people. "Yes!" he said, raising his arms exactly like Thomas. "That's the coolest thing God's ever let me do!" he whispered excitedly. "That's awesome!"

I couldn't stop tears from coming to my eyes. I felt relief and happiness that had nothing to do with the huge crush I had on Micah. I used the paper napkin that was sitting on my lap to wipe the happy tears, and the next thing I knew he was out of his chair standing next to me.

He stuck out his hand and I took it, letting him pull me up and into his arms. He hugged me tightly. "Thank you for letting me be a part of this," he said, although I wasn't quite sure if he was talking to me or God. "Are you finished?" he asked, breaking the hug and gesturing at my unfinished salad.

I nodded and smiled, and picked up our baskets. "Come on, there's a park across the street. We can walk around for a little bit before I take you back to your car."

We did just that.

It wasn't a huge park. There were two playground structures and an open field that a soccer team was using for practice. There was a paved walking path circling the perimeter, and we went around it three or four times.

The soccer team got us talking about sports. I told him I played softball and did ballet as a kid, but

160

wasn't serious with either of them. He was more of an athlete. He said he played soccer during both high school and college. I joked that he should join the practicing team to prove his skills, but he just smiled and said he didn't want to put them to shame.

Halloween had just passed, and he asked me what I dressed up as. I told him I went to school as Einstein, which made him ask me to show me a picture. I took out my phone and let him flip through a few photos we'd taken that day. Micah marveled at how good my costume was. It was actually pretty convincing. Trish helped me with it, and all the students went crazy over how much I looked like him. They even made me take a picture with my tongue out like the famous one of Einstein for the yearbook. I showed Micah that one too, and he cracked up, saying I was the coolest teacher ever.

He had me laughing the entire time we walked. He was smart, and his quick wit and dry humor kept me on my toes. I appreciated him not making too big of a deal about me accepting Christ. It was a big deal to me, but for some reason it made me feel good that he assumed I could go on with life as usual. I guess I just assumed he would give me a long list of things I should and shouldn't do, and was relieved when that didn't happen.

We walked slowly, and shared enjoyable, easy conversation the whole time. The longer we were together, the more I ached for physical contact. I was so drawn to him that I wanted to ask him to put his

arm around my shoulder or something. Anything—
even an accidental brush of the arms would have
offered some relief, but it didn't happen.

We walked, talked, glanced at each other,
smiled, and laughed, but not once did he touch me. I
probably shouldn't have been concerned about
something like that on a night when my soul was
eternally saved, but I couldn't help it. I felt like I was
being drawn to him like a magnet.

He asked me a lot about science and my teaching
job at Roosevelt, and I asked him about the ins and
outs of the concrete business. We strolled around
that park for what must have been about an hour. It
was probably the best hour of my life, but I knew I
had to get home, and I told him so.

"Are you up for some dessert?" he asked on our
way back to his truck.

"I wish I could. I have to get home to Roscoe,
and I have some last minute planning to do for
school tomorrow. Thank you, though, and thank you
for dinner."

"I want to take you on a real date sometime, if
you're okay with that," he said.

"What's a real date, exactly?"

We climbed into his truck, and he regarded me
from over the console with an irresistible smile. *Had
Micah Bennett just said he wanted to take me on a
date?* I felt like I was living in some alternate reality.

"One where we plan it ahead of time, and I pick
you up at your house. We can sit at a real restaurant

and have someone take our order, and most importantly, there will be no promises of staying away from scientific research."

"Oh really?" I asked.

He started the engine and began driving. "Yeah, I'm sort of upset about making that stupid promise tonight, if you want to know the truth."

I laughed. "I don't know how I feel about going out on a date with a Christian," I said.

He glanced at me to find that I was wearing an expression of mock distaste, which made him laugh. "I guess I'll just have to go out with Gina, then," he said.

"Awww, that was low," I said, laughing.

"Why's it low?" he asked with a shrug, teasing me. "I was just randomly thinking of someone who'd be happy to go out on a date with me despite my beliefs."

"Oh, and you just randomly thought of her," I said.

He glanced at me to find that my eyebrows were raised in a look of challenge.

"Are you jealous?" he asked.

Of course I was jealous. I was jealous of any girl in the universe who could possibly stand in the way of me being with Micah. My heart was completely set on happily ever after with him, and every moment between now and then seemed somehow both crucial and wasted at the same time.

"Does it mean I'm jealous if I'd much rather you take me on a date than her?" I asked, finally finding the nerve to say something halfway sincere. I cringed inwardly as I waiting for his response.

"I don't think that classifies you as jealous," he said, "but I think somewhere in there you might have just agreed to a date."

"I guess I did," I said.

"What about Friday?"

"This Friday?" I asked.

"No, three Fridays from now—of course this Friday!"

"I think that'll be good," I said.

"Do you need to check your schedule and get back with me?" he asked in a teasing tone.

"No..." I said, "I'm pretty sure I'm open this Friday."

It only took us another minute to get back to the Happy House. He parked on the street right behind my car, put his truck in park, and looked at me.

"I guess you need my number so you can get in touch with me if something comes up," I said. I got my phone out of my bag and got to the screen that prompted me to add a contact. I typed in the name M-i-c-a-h, trying to contain a smile the whole time. "Okay give me your number and I'll call you so you'll have mine."

He recited his number and I pushed the call button.

He nodded. "I hear it buzzing," he said, even though I didn't hear anything.

I stared at him for a few seconds before speaking. "Thanks again for everything tonight" I said. I could feel warmth rise to my cheeks at the sincere words that came out of my mouth.

"Thank you," he said. "I had such a great time."

I smiled. "Me too."

"You better go," he said, "because the longer you're in here, the more tempted I am to break my promise about not making you work."

I wanted to make him break that promise so badly I could barely contain myself. I wanted nothing more than for Micah Bennett to put his mouth on mine again. I wanted it so badly I almost couldn't make words come out. I had to clear my throat before I could speak.

"Maybe I'll feel like working Friday," I said, torturing myself for the sake of not being too eager. I smiled at him as I opened the door. I could tell by the look on his face that he was as tempted as I was, and that pleased me greatly.

"Goodnight, Carly," he said.

"Goodnight, Micah."

I hopped out of the truck, giving him one last smile before I closed the door.

I had my car door open and was just about to sit down when he yelled, "Carly wait!" I turned to see that he'd stepped out of his truck and was walking toward me. I took in his long, confident stride wondering if a more beautiful, masculine creature had ever been created.

He smiled as he approached me, tossing his hands into the air as he got close. "I thought I was an honest man," he said. "I thought I could make a promise and keep it, but I was sitting there in my truck, watching you walk off, and I just couldn't take it anymore." He paused. "I'm sorry," he said. "I know I said I wouldn't kiss you tonight, but I'm not going to be able to keep that promise—I just can't do it."

"You can't?" I asked, staring up at him breathless. He shook his head as he looked into my eyes, stepping closer.

"Do you forgive me?" he asked.

All I had to do was nod once and his hand came around the back of my head. His lips fell onto mine in another painfully gentle kiss. A rush of warmth coursed through my body as my heart raced wildly.

"Carly?" he whispered with is lips still touching mine.

"Huh?" I asked.

He pulled back just far enough to focus on me. "Please tell me you think the experiment worked this time."

I nodded.

"Did you think it worked last time too?"

I let the hint of a smile touch my mouth as I nodded again.

"How about this time?" he asked. He used the hand on the back of my head to pull me towards him again, and I went willingly. He put his lips on mine again. It was chaste, but it had me weak in the knees.

"Uh-huh," I said, weakly.

"Okay," he whispered. He let go of me. "I'm sorry I didn't keep my promise."

"It's all right," I said.

"So, I'll see you Friday?" he asked, turning to retreat to his truck.

I smiled—or at least I tried to. "Yep."

I was getting in my car when he yelled at me from his truck. "Hey Carly?"

"Yeah?"

I watched his gorgeous form as he swung open the door to his truck with a smile. "I'm proud of you for that decision you made earlier. Thanks for letting me be a part of that."

I didn't want to say you're welcome, and I felt too shy to say thank you back, so I smiled shyly and waved before getting into my car.

Chapter 16

There was nothing I could do to wipe the huge grin off of my face. I felt as if I had fallen in love twice in the same night. Happiness and hope just oozed out of me.

Trish, Ryan, and Isaac were all in plain sight when I came home. Isaac was on the couch watching TV, and Trish and Ryan were in the kitchen. Roscoe ran to greet me at the door with his tail wagging like crazy.

"Ryan brought home a new coffee maker," Trish said, "and we're trying to figure it out."

"They've been in there for an hour," Isaac chimed in from the couch.

I glanced at Trish who shot me a look of frustration. "We can't figure out how to make it use this reusable pod, and there's no way we're buying the prefilled cups all the time."

"They want to make it hard, so we have to buy them," Ryan said. He looked at me. "Also, Trish gave Roscoe half of her burrito."

Trish slapped at him and gave him an open-mouthed look of shock. "I can't believe you're telling on me! You're the one who gives him a dog biscuit every time you walk into the kitchen."

I'd already taken off my shoes and purse and had made my way into the living room. I laughed as I bent to pet Roscoe again. "They're gonna make you out of shape, boy," I said. "We're gonna have to go to the doggy gym."

Isaac, who was a total fitness nut and spent most of his free time in a gym, cracked up laughing at the thought. I plopped onto the couch beside Isaac and Roscoe jumped up to sit on my lap.

"What took you so long?" Trish asked from the kitchen. "I went to dinner after I taught that class."

I looked at her to find that she was staring at me with raised eyebrows, which made me smile. My face literally hurt from smiling so much. "Did you go to dinner with that guyyyy?" she asked, teasing me.

My smile only broadened.

"You gotta new boyfriend?" Ryan asked.

"He's not my boyfriend, but he did buy my dinner," I hesitated. "And he might have kissed me."

Ryan and Trish both made sounds of approval from the kitchen. Isaac didn't say anything, but he lifted his eyebrow suggestively when I glanced his way.

"Who is this guy?" Ryan asked.

"His name's Micah," I said.

"She's had a crush on him for five years," Trish added.

"You make it sound like I'm a stalker or something," I defended. "I pretty much forgot about him for about four and a half of those years."

"Isaac's got a new lady friend too," Trish said.

"What is this, sharing time?" Isaac said, looking annoyed.

"Why are you being so shy?" Trish said. "I saw her when you two came by the other day and she's gorgeous."

"Yeah, but I don't know if I'd call her my lady friend just yet."

"Oh come on, if I can tease Carly, then I can tease you too."

He looked at Trish. "As long as we're teasing, how about those eight inch heels you had on when you went out with Shane the other night? You could barely walk in those things."

Everyone laughed including Trish. She seriously could barely walk.

"I almost broke my ankle in those things," Trish said, being a good sport. "Come to think of it, Isaac, your lady friend had on some pretty tall shoes as well. She was stiff-toeing it around this whole house just like me."

Isaac didn't quite see the humor in that, but the rest of us cracked up.

I sat in the living room talking with my roommates for about 30 more minutes before I excused myself to shower and do my lesson planning. I came really close to telling them about my decision to follow Christ, but I couldn't find the right moment to bring it up. Regardless of the fact that I didn't talk about it, it was on the forefront of my mind. I saw this allergy commercial once where everything was dull and hazy, and after the person took the allergy pill, the world became brighter and more clear. That's what I felt like. Everything around me was the same, I just saw it differently. It was like I was looking at the world through hope-tinted glasses, and it felt great.

I thought about Zeke and the incident that night as I did most every night when I laid in my dark room, but I thought about what Micah said. I thought God had let me experience that as a part of a greater plan, and peace fell on me like a warm blanket.

***

The next day was Thursday, and I decided to go to the gym. Isaac had been bugging me to do so, and my upcoming date with Micah was just the motivation I needed. I knew that one trip to the gym wouldn't change anything, but it still felt good to go. I was proud of myself for doing it, and felt so pumped on the way home that, by the time I pulled up in my driveway, I decided to text Micah.

Me: "Just wanted to say hi and thanks again for yesterday."

I pressed send but instantly regretted it. *Why couldn't I have just waited till tomorrow?* I stashed my phone in my purse and went inside, regretting that rash decision. *How desperate.*

I ate dinner and showered without looking at my phone. It was when I finally sat on the couch to watch TV that I got the nerve to check it. I saw when I first opened it that I had a message from Micah. I got hit with a wave of adrenaline as I opened it and began to read.

Micah: "I had a blast. Can't wait for tomorrow."

He'd sent it only a minute after I sent mine earlier. I stared at it, wondering if I should text him back. Trish and her boyfriend had been hanging out in her room, and they came out into the living just as I was trying to decide what I should do.

I ended up talking to them for a little while, and somewhere in our conversation I asked their opinion on whether or not I should text Micah back. We had a long, hilarious discussion about texting etiquette at the beginning of a relationship. Trish and Shane we're still at the very start of their relationship, so it was funny to see their dynamics as they spoke about it.

Ultimately, I decided to text him back.

Me: "I'm stoked about it. Where are you taking me?"

I did not want to ask a direct question that obligated him to text me back, but Shane and Trish both told me to do it and okayed the text before I sent it. My phone vibrated instantly and I glanced at them with wide-eyed excitement as I picked it up.

Micah: "I'm not telling you, but it's not that I don't have a plan, because I do. Also, I got you something."

I read the text out loud to them and they high-fived each other. "This is a done deal," Trish said, nodding confidently.

"What's that supposed to mean?" I asked.

"It means you don't need our advice." She gestured to my phone. "You got the guy buying you stuff. I don't think you really need to worry about composing the right text."

Shane nodded. "Yeah, guys don't go out and buy stuff for just anybody," he said.

"Shane's never bought me anything," Trish said.

He looked ashamed and reached out to tickle her. "Let's go to the store right now," he said.

She squirmed and giggled. "It's not romantic if I pick it out," she said still laughing. "You have to do it by yourself like Carly's boyfriend."

I almost corrected her for saying boyfriend, but I didn't since I liked the sound of it.

Micah picked me up at 7pm on the dot the following evening. My roommates all had plans, so I was the only one home when he got there. He looked amazing as usual in a pair of dark jeans, hiking boots, and a light green long-sleeve button up shirt that made his eyes all but glow. I was wearing a dark green sweater and he joked about us having on our team uniforms.

He came in and met Roscoe who took to him instantly. He only stayed for a minute, though, because we were both starving and ready to get to the restaurant. I showed him the framed picture of the treasure chest Thomas painted before I put Roscoe in his kennel and locked the house. Then we made our way to his truck.

He started the engine, but didn't put it in gear. I watched as he dug in the pocket of the driver's side door. "You might have one of these, but I wanted to pick it up anyway," he said. He handed me an unwrapped box that contained a Bible. I glanced at him and he shrugged shyly. "I just got it in case you didn't have one already. You can take it back if you don't think you'll use it."

I opened the box, and inside there was a small, leather bound book. I took it out and held it in my hand. The leather was soft, and I could tell it was well made. It felt alive in my hands, and I remembered all the things Thomas said about it five years before when I first met him. Tears rose to my eyes as I stared down at it. It was the best gift he could have possibly chosen. I flipped through it, staring down at the pages.

"It's perfect," I said.

"You like it?"

I set it back in its box and looked at him. "I love it," I said. "I don't have one, and it's exactly the one I would have chosen for myself."

"Oh I'm so glad," he said He started the truck. "God will speak to you through that thing. There's a ton of stuff in there that will help you if you catch yourself having a rough time with memories or whatever."

I closed it and set it on the console between us. "That was really thoughtful," I said. "Thank you."

He reached over to touch my arm in a gesture that said you're welcome. It was like he meant to touch me and take his hand away instantly but he couldn't quite go through with pulling his hand back. He let his fingertips linger on my arm for a few seconds before taking it off, and during those seconds, an electrical charge pulsed through my body. I found it difficult to think or breathe. He turned on the radio, and I was thankful for that because I was seriously struggling to catch my breath.

He took me to a really nice restaurant called Velvet Meg's. I had heard of it before. Meg White was a well-known chef who had starred on a few reality shows on Food Network. It usually took a while to get reservations at her restaurant, but Micah said his dad's construction company did most of the work on the place, so he and Meg had become friends.

We talked about our families as we ate. I told him my parents had divorced when I was young, and my dad had fallen off the map with my stepmom and her family. They still lived in San Antonio, but I rarely saw them and thought of my mom and stepdad as my family unit. His parents had been together all his life, so he didn't have any divorce stories, but he had plenty of funny stories about growing up—especially with Thomas.

We had a nice, goodhearted laugh talking about how Thomas would stop midsentence and begin to wail if something touched his heart. He made it clear how much he loved his brother, which made me feel good because I loved him too.

Towards the end of our meal, Chef Meg came out of the kitchen to greet us herself. I had seen her on Food Network, and it was neat to see the familiarity between them. He introduced me and we had a short but sweet conversation before she excused herself to get back to the kitchen. Micah was smart and well spoken, and I found myself being proud of him during our conversation with her.

We were headed out to the parking lot when he took his phone out of his pocket. "I'm sorry, but I should take this. It's a client, and it's the third time she's called."

I nodded, and he put the phone to his ear. I listened to his one sided conversation.

"Hello."

"Yes ma'am."

"That's okay. I was out to dinner. Is everything okay?"

"Are we still on for Monday?"

"Oh, no ma'am. Please don't go to all that trouble. It'll just be me and a few of my crew, and we always bring lunch or get something quick."

"No, no, I don't want you to have to do that. If you feed my men too good, I might not be able to get them to work."

"We'll be done by Wednesday or Thursday, but it'll need to cure before the stain goes on."

He glanced at me and shook his head regretfully.

"Okay, if you insist, I'm sure they'll be thankful for a home cooked lunch, but please don't put yourself out. We're used to bringing a sandwich."

"Okay thanks. I'll tell 'em not to bring their lunch on Monday."

"We'll see you then."

"Okay, bye."

We were sitting in his truck by the time he finished the conversation, and he shot me an *I'm sorry* expression.

"That was one of my clients wanting to see if I would eat pork chops and mashed potatoes for lunch on Monday."

"Must be nice," I said. "I wish my students knew how to whip up a home cooked meal for me sometime."

"That's not an everyday thing," he said. "They just happen to be extremely attentive clients. It's like the fifth time they've called, and the job hasn't even started." He smiled and lifted a shoulder. "They go to our church." Then he made a face like he remembered something and smiled regretfully. "I think you know them, actually."

"Gina?" I asked, knowing exactly who it was by the look on his face.

"Yeah, the Youngs. I'm doing a big patio and some pavers at their house next week. Ms. Cathy said she and Gina wanted to make lunch for us everyday, but I can't have that. I'd never get my guys to finish the job if they fed us everyday."

He glanced at me and I smiled as sweetly as I could even though I was suddenly nauseated.

Chapter 17

I prayed to God right then. I prayed God would forgive me for the super bad thoughts I had about Gina Young.

I pictured Micah doing manly stuff in Gina's backyard with her serving him ice-cold lemonade on a tray. She'd probably be all dolled up like some perfect little homemaker while I was stuck in 11th grade science class explaining the principals of science to a student who could care less, or trying to talk some angsty teenage girl off a ledge about her boyfriend during my office hour.

I was lost in thought picturing the whole terrible scenario when he said, "Do you skate?" I stared at him from the passenger's side, wondering if I'd heard him right.

He was watching the road, so I was staring at the side of his face when I asked, "Did you just ask if I skate?"

He laughed at the way I said it. "Yeah."

"Roller skate?" I asked.

He glanced at me with a smile. "Uh-huh. I was gonna take you there, but I figured I should ask first since that's sort of a random place for a date."

"Do *you* skate?" I asked, still thrown off.

He seemed amused by my reluctance. "I'm not a professional or anything, but I can get around the rink without falling as long as no one pushes me over or anything."

"You want to bring me roller skating?" I asked.

He shrugged and glanced at me again. "I thought it'd be fun. But we definitely don't have to if you're not up for it. I think there are a few good bands playing tonight, or we can see a movie."

I'd been so caught up with the way Gina had somehow managed to interrupt our date, that I had to remind myself to stop freaking out and enjoy the evening. He was, after all on a date with me.

"I might have gone to Skate City every Friday night of my life for about three years straight," I said.

"Are you trying to say you're good?" he asked, smirking at me.

"I'm not the type to brag," I said, obviously talking some smack.

He laughed. "We're going," he said.

The skating rink we went to wasn't the same one I went to as a kid, but if you've been to one of them, you've been to all of them. Familiar sights, sounds, and smells hit me the instant we walked through the door.

It was odd to go on a real date where a guy took out his wallet everywhere we went and paid my way. I hadn't dated anyone since Zeke, and even then, he didn't pay for anything. It felt surreal, like I was in a movie or something. I thanked him for paying my way and we took our tickets up to the counter to exchange them for a pair of skates. I got a 7 and he got an 11, and we brought them to the carpet covered benches that lined the rink so we could put them on.

We passed an arcade along the way that had Skee-Ball machines, so of course I made him promise to let me play before we left. A whole host of memories flooded my mind as I sat down and stared out onto the rink. It was full of people of all ages—some which could skate well, and others that could barely stay on their feet.

"This is the coolest idea ever," I said, glancing at him. "I haven't done it in like ten years, but I'm so excited."

"It's been a while for me too," he said, "so we might have to hang onto each other at first."

My heart skipped a beat at the mention of hanging onto each other. I was so dialed in to the anticipation of his touch, that I wanted to swoon at the very thought of it. I did my best to appear less nervous than I was.

I put on the skates and laced them up tightly. I finished before him, so I stood and tried them out on the carpeted area where we were sitting. "How's it feel?" he asked.

"Good... on carpet," I said. "We'll see how it goes on that slickness." I turned and watched the action on the rink as he finished, and before I knew it, he was standing next to me.

"Ready?" he asked, smiling down at me.

I was extremely glad that I had some fairly good skating skills because Micah held his own out there. He didn't do any fancy stuff, but he was loose and agile for such a big guy, and I would have felt like a big dork if he showed me up after what I said in the truck. Unfortunately, he did not need to lean on me for balance. Part of me hoped there'd be some necessary physical contact, but that wasn't the case.

The DJ was playing pop music. As a high school teacher, I not only recognized but also knew most of the songs by heart. By the time we were 10 laps in, I was steady enough on my feet to dance around and sing a little bit, which obviously entertained Micah.

His smile was so mesmerizing that I was compelled to say, "I think I'm with the cutest guy here."

Micah looked around as if assessing the competition.

"I would totally be jealous of me if I were any other girl here."

"Nobody even knows we're here together," he said, tossing his hands into the air.

I didn't understand his comment and it made me narrow my eyes at him. "What do you mean? We've been skating together the whole time."

"Yeah, but anybody can skate next to anybody," he said. "If we were really here together, we'd be holding hands."

"Oh, so you're saying my options are open?" I asked, looking around.

"I'm saying I want to hold your hand."

My heart either stopped beating all together, or started beating so fast that I couldn't tell the difference. *Remain cool. Remain cool.* I casually held my hand in his direction as if it was okay with me if he took it, and that's just what he did. He laced his fingers in mine, and I might as well have been in middle school with all the butterflies that were churning in my stomach. His hand was big and warm and he rubbed his thumb on the back of my hand as if enjoying the feel of my skin. It was all I could do to remember to skate.

"You slowed down," he said, to my horror. It was true. We had skated an entire lap at about half speed since he grabbed my hand.

"I'm almost forgetting to skate," I said, feeling like I should just be honest.

I glanced at him and he shot me a breathtaking smile. "Because you like holding my hand?" he asked.

"A little bit," I said.

"I think you might like me," he said.

If only he knew.

"I might," I said casually.

"I might have to take you out again," he said.

I smiled at him. "You might."

We skated for over an hour, talking about anything and everything under the sun. We brought up church, and I told him I thought I might want to try to go with him sometime, but I didn't want to cramp his style. He laughed at me for saying that and told me he thought it would be weird if I went anywhere else.

We discussed food, travel, art, movies, and random things like the fact that he had a broken arm at the age of 12 from falling out of a tree. We both agreed that we would probably be sore from using skate-related muscle groups and decided it was time to call it a night.

It was 10:00 when he pulled up in my driveway. He put his truck in park and I turned to him with a smile. "I should probably act more aloof than this," I said, "but I'll go ahead and tell you that I had a super awesome time tonight. Seriously, thank you for being the most fun guy ever and for paying for all my stuff. I loved everything."

He stared at me with an unreadable smile as if he was trying to figure me out even though I was putting it all out there.

"And thank you for the Bible," I added, taking it from the console.

"That reminds me. I have something for Roscoe."

"You do?"

He reached into the door pocket and pulled up a small bag of those teeth cleaning bones. "I wanted to get him the big dinosaur bone, but the lady at the pet store said he'd love these and they were good for him."

"He does," I said. "Do you want to give it to him yourself?"

"Now that you mention it," he said, as if he was just waiting for me to ask.

I giggled as we both climbed out of the truck. I knew Isaac was home because his car was in the driveway, but Ryan and Trish were both gone. The door was unlocked, and Micah followed me inside. We took off our shoes and left them by the door.

"I'll be right back," I said, going to my room to let Roscoe out of his kennel.

"Is that you, Carly?" Isaac yelled from his room.

"Yeah, it's me." I yelled back.

"I just got home a few minutes ago. I was just about to let him out."

Isaac's room was the closest to the living room, and he must've heard me come in.

"Thanks!" I yelled back through his closed door. "I got it."

I talked to Roscoe the whole time as I carefully placed my beautiful new Bible on the nightstand and then opened his kennel. He was extremely excited to see me as always. "You better go get your treat from Micah," I said. He didn't listen to me, though. He just stood at my feet waiting for love with his tail whipping around in circles. I patted my leg as I headed to the living room. "Come on, boy."

Roscoe followed me out there. Micah called him over when we entered, and Roscoe ran to him and sprang onto the couch.

"Is he allowed to be up here?" Micah asked, looking at me. I nodded, and Micah patted his lap. Roscoe was a pro at lap sitting, and he curled up on Micah's legs the instant he was invited. Micah shot me a *can you believe this* look that I answered with a smile.

"He's a lover," I said, shrugging.

"It's no wonder Thomas loves him," Micah said, petting him. "I need to get him one of these."

I crossed the room and sat on the couch next to them, reaching over to ensure Roscoe he was okay in his current position when he thought about creeping over to me. We sat like that for a minute until Micah gave Roscoe one of the bones. He jumped down, and carried it to the kitchen where he devoured it before coming back to the couch to sit with us.

He settled between us but was only there for a second before Isaac came out of his room and Roscoe jumped down to greet him.

"Hey my boy," Isaac said affectionately as he stooped down to pet him. Isaac worked extremely hard on his body, and was proud of the results. He almost never wore a shirt if he could avoid it. He came into the living room wearing nothing but sweat pants that hung low on his hips, and the sight of him made Micah sit up straight.

"Oh, hey, I didn't know you had somebody with you," Isaac said, noticing Micah for the first time as he stood.

I patted the couch next to me and Roscoe jumped on it again. Isaac took a step toward Micah with an outstretched hand, and Micah stood to shake it.

"Isaac, this is my friend Micah," I said. "Micah, this is my roommate, Isaac."

They greeted each other with a firm handshake and a nod the way guys do.

"Are you guys going to be out here for a while?" Isaac asked, trying to gauge whether or not we wanted privacy.

I shook my head. "Micah just came in to give Roscoe some toothbrush bones. We went skating tonight... Can you believe that?"

"I got him one of those bones the other day," Isaac said, ignoring my skating comment. "He loves them."

"Did you hear me say we went skating?" I asked, incredulous.

Isaac smiled at me. "Roller skating?"

"Yes, roller skating! And we were both really good! All the kids were looking at us like *whaaat*?"

He laughed and rolled his eyes at me like I was the silliest thing ever, and then he crossed to the kitchen and started searching in a cabinet for a glass. He sat at the bar and spaced out on his phone for a few minutes while Micah and I continued our conversation.

"You wanna walk me out?" Micah asked, finally.

"Are you leaving?"

"Yeah, I guess I should."

We stood and Micah looked toward the kitchen. "It was nice meeting you, Isaac," he said.

Isaac pulled out his earbuds with a smile and wave in Micah's direction. "Nice meeting you too."

I peered down at Roscoe, who was standing at our feet, wagging his tail as if asking where we were going. "You're staying here," I said. He obviously didn't understand because he followed us to the door and was disappointed when I shut it with him inside.

Micah and I walked to his truck, and I turned to face him when we reached it. His expression was serious and questioning at the same time. "Is that something that happens all the time?" he asked tentatively.

I smiled and nodded. "Oh, yeah! Basically, all you have to do is sit down and pat your lap, and he jumps up there."

Micah closed his eyes and cringed slightly. "Please tell me you're talking about the dog," he said.

I looked at him with a confused expression. "Who were *you* talking about?"

"You're shirtless roommate," he said, gesturing to the house. "Does he walk around like that all the time?"

I leaned against his truck and regarded him with a sly smile. "Are you jealous?" I asked.

188

He closed the distance between us, coming to stand only inches from me. He rested his arm on the truck, letting it brush against my shoulder. He stared down at me with an intense, barely-there smile as if taking in every centimeter of my face.

"I don't even know how to answer that question," he said. "I don't know if I'd call it jealous, but the thought of you going back into that house with a half naked man makes me feel..." he hesitated, staring into the empty space next to my head and rubbing his jaw as of searching for the right word. "...Uh, crazy? Insane?"

I thought he was mostly joking, and I laughed and squirmed, feeling delighted that he even cared enough to mention it.

He cupped his hand under my chin, tilting it up so I'd look at him. He gave me another small smile, but shook his head and said, "I'm not kidding, Carly. The thought of you going back in there with him dressed like that makes me... not happy. Does he walk around like that all the time?"

Chapter 18

I flinched at the thought of how frequently Isaac walked around the house shirtless. It was literally all the time. I almost never saw him with a shirt on unless he was headed out the door.

Micah must have sensed my hesitation because he repeated his question. "Does he walk around like that all the time?" he asked again.

I tried to keep my face emotionless, but it was incredibly difficult. Micah was obviously annoyed by the thought, and that made me overwhelmingly happy. I wondered if he was as annoyed by Isaac as I was by the thought of him getting home cooked meals at Gina's house.

"He just likes to show off because he works so hard at the gym," I said, carefully avoiding the question.

Micah blew out a long, exasperated breath and shook his head, looking off to the side as if extremely irritated by the thought. I watched the muscles in his jaw and temple flex as I stared at his profile.

"I have abs too," he said, glancing down at me, still agitated. "But you don't see me letting them all hang out."

"You have abs?" I asked, unable to hide my amusement as I smiled up at him.

He furrowed his eyebrows at me, and I bit my lip to keep from smiling too hard. Before I knew what was happening, he took my hand and placed it on his stomach. I could feel how solid and rigid his abs were, even with a layer of fabric between us. My breath hitched and my amused grin faded as my heart started beating out of control. He smiled at the sight of my sudden shift, and his smile only served to make me more breathless.

"You do have abs," I said.

"Yeah, I have abs," he said confidently, "and I work hard on them just like your roommate in there, but you don't see me walking around without a shirt all the time, do you?"

I wanted to say I wish you would, but I held my tongue.

"And I don't know how I feel about him being all, *that's my boy* with Roscoe, and giving him treats and all that."

Another huge smile spread across my face, and I had to try to hold it back a little. Isaac, in no way shape or form, held a candle to Micah, but I couldn't help but take pleasure in seeing him so annoyed.

"What's so funny?" he asked, scowling at me. "How would you feel if I was going home to a half naked woman right now?"

"I'm not *going home* to him," I defended. "I barely even notice him. He's just my roommate. He's seeing somebody, anyway."

He let out a huff. "All the more reason he needs to put on a shirt," he said.

His hand had been holding mine against his stomach as we talked, and at that point, he let them drop, but didn't let go of my hand. I was hyper aware of his touch, and nerves continually coursed through my body. He readjusted his hand to get a better grip on mine and I stared at him not knowing what to say. We stood that way for several long seconds, just checking each other out before he finally spoke again.

"It's probably stupid for me to get so mad, but here's the way I look at it..." he hesitated, and sighed as if looking for the right words. "Okay, so way back when the accident first happened, I was pretty much a mess. I had all this guilt, resentment, doubt, and anger. I was trying to give it to God, and knew that He would use it for my good, but it was just overwhelming, you know?"

He paused, and I nodded. A little smile touched his lips, and I clutched his hand in both of mine, feeling like I wanted to comfort him.

"Well, during the absolute worst time," he continued, "when I was in the freaking pit of despair, God clearly spoke to me. It wasn't an audible voice, but it was one of those clear feelings where I knew beyond a shadow of a doubt that it came from God. Anyway, what He told me was that someday I'd find someone who understood my pain."

He paused with a shy smile.

"So I held on to that, and when you told me your story, I knew that was it. I knew it was you. Getting to know you only confirms it."

He pulled his hand out of mine and used it to tuck my hair behind my ear.

"What I'm trying to say is that in my mind, you're mine. I know we're just getting to know each other, and I probably shouldn't have told you any of this so soon, but my brain thinks of you belonging to me. You're supposed to be mine." He gestured toward my house again. "So maybe that'll help you understand why I'm about ready to kill Fabio in there if he doesn't put a shirt on and leave my dog alone."

His statement made me giggle. I was already feeling giddy, and his reference to Roscoe as his dog put me over the edge. I blinked up at him to find that he was smiling too.

"I don't mean to scare you with any of that, I just thought it might explain why I—"

"I'm not scared," I said, cutting him off.

I gently put my hand on his cheek because I just couldn't resist touching it any longer. My fingertips grazed the edge of his scar, and in that second, I thanked God for the pain we had both been through.

"I'm going to kiss you now," he said.

"Please," I whispered breathlessly.

His mouth came down on mine with an absence of gentleness. He wasn't rough with me, but he meant this kiss. He wrapped one arm around my waist and the other around the back of my head, as he clutched me firmly to him. I opened to him, and he dipped his tongue into my mouth several times, claiming me as his own. My legs were rendered useless, and he held my limp body as he kissed me deeply.

I let out an uncontrollable moan, which made him break the kiss. He pulled back and we stared at each other breathlessly as if wondering what had just happened.

"I'm sorry," he said. "No, I'm not actually, but if you want me to be, I'll say I am."

"I don't want you to be sorry," I said.

"You want me to do it again?" he asked, challengingly.

I nodded and he bent to kiss me again, only this time he used extreme constraint, which drove me equally as crazy. He held me by the back of the head as he placed kiss after gentle kiss on my mouth, cheek, jaw, neck, and then back up to my mouth again. I let out another small moan and he pulled back to stare down at me again.

"Yeah, you're not gonna be able to make that sound," he said.

"What sound?" I asked, not even realizing what I'd done. "That whimper or whatever that was. I don't think I can handle that kind of temptation."

"I whimpered?" I asked, laughing at myself.

"It's a good sound, baby girl," he said, squeezing me. "It's a little too good if you know what I mean."

"I'm sorry," I said, feeling embarrassed.

"How about neither of us be sorry," he said.

He had just bent to kiss my cheek when headlights shone brightly on us. Micah let go of the grip he had on me, but kept his hand loosely on the back of my waist. One of my roommates was home, and a few seconds of focusing on the car after they turned the engine off told me it was Ryan.

"Sorry!" Ryan called, getting out of his car. He approached us on his way into the house. He was just getting off work from his job waiting tables, and he was sharply dressed in all black. "You think you can get out?" Ryan asked, glancing back at his own parking job.

"Yeah, I can make it," Micah said.

Ryan smiled at him. "Hey, man, I'm Ryan," he said, holding his hand out.

Micah shook his hand without letting go of me. "Micah," he said, smiling.

"It's nice to meet you," Ryan said. He glanced at me and lifted the small paper sack he was holding. "I brought a little piece of pork roast for Roscoe, can I give it to him?"

"Only if it's little," I said. "He just had a treat. If it's too big you can give it to him tomorrow."

"I'll break off a little bite for him tonight if you don't care."

"That's fine. Thanks, Ryan."

Ryan waved at Micah again who answered with a smile and a curt nod.

"Are you kidding me?" Micah asked when Ryan made his way inside. He looked down at me with a challenging expression that made me laugh.

"They're just my roommates," I said.

"I thought Trish was your roommate."

"She is."

"Does he walk around naked too?" he asked, motioning to the door.

I giggled. "Isaac wasn't naked."

Micah was wearing a gorgeous, casual smile but he said, "Please understand this is not an ideal situation for me."

"Well please understand that they're just my roommates and nothing more," I said.

"Fair enough," he said, still wearing a little grin. "I guess I better be going."

I wanted to ask when I'd see or talk to him again. I felt a strong urge to never be apart from him, and the thought of him leaving had me dreading the void he'd leave in his wake.

"Don't forget to come to science class if you want to see the Coke experiment," I said, hoping to make a definite time to see him again so I could look forward to it.

"I'll see you before then," he said.

"Oh." I paused. "You will?"

"I thought I'd probably see you tomorrow, but if you can't, I figured you might want to come with us to church on Sunday. I'm filling in for the praise and worship guy this week. I'll be singing during both services, so I'll be there all morning."

"You're singing?" I asked.

He smiled and gave me a nod. "You coming?"

"I might," I said, "but I might need some more convincing when I see you tomorrow."

He smiled and pulled me by the waist into his embrace. He bent and placed one last kiss on my mouth. It felt like heaven, and I wanted to moan, but I made a conscious effort not to. I was smiling at the thought when he let me go.

"What?" he asked.

"Nothin'," I said, still grinning slightly. "I had fun tonight. Thanks for everything."

He opened the door of his truck and stood there, poised to get in. "I'll call you in the morning," he said.

I nodded and held up a hand to wave. I felt like I wanted to tell him *I love you.* I didn't want him to drive off without hearing it from me, but I knew that was ridiculous, so I just stood there and smiled as he got in his truck and backed out of the driveway.

He rolled down his window to wave one last time before driving off, and I turned to go into the house feeling like I was walking on clouds. *He's calling me in the morning; he's calling me in the morning,* I thought, grinning uncontrollably as I opened the door.

Isaac was in the living room watching TV, but Ryan must have been in his room. "Ryan wanted me to tell you he needed fifteen minutes in the shower before you could run any hot water," Isaac said, not looking away from the TV.

"That's fine," I said, stooping to love on Roscoe.

Isaac looked at me. "And he gave Roscoe a big ole hunkin' pork chop."

"Did he really?" I asked.

Isaac smiled. "No, he gave him a little piece. I'm just messing with you."

"You're spoiled rotten," I said, still petting Roscoe, who had rolled onto his back for a belly rub.

"I can't believe you went roller skating," Isaac said. "Your quads and hammys are gonna be feeling that tomorrow."

I laughed. "I already told Micah that," I said. "It was so worth it, though." I stared into space as I remembered the highlights of this night. "I also ate at Velvet Meg's and I got to meet the chef."

"Seriously?" he asked, looking impressed.

"Yeah, Micah's family knows her."

"He seems nice," he said.

I let out a long, enamored sigh.

"Uh-oh," he said. "That sounds like trouble."

I let out a little laugh. "I'm in so much trouble," I agreed. "You have no idea."

Chapter 19

I picked up the Bible Micah gave me when I climbed into bed. The cover was soft, but the pages were stiff and unyielding, and I imagined it all broken in after years of use.

I looked down at it, not really knowing where to begin. I thought about opening it and starting to read on the first page but ultimately decided to thumb through it, letting my eye fall on random places here and there. It seemed a bit mysterious to me, but I found myself being drawn to it. I read for a while before I set it on my nightstand and turned off my lamp, letting my head hit the pillow with a comfortable whoosh.

I had a hard time going to sleep that night. I stared at the ceiling, thinking about our date and reliving the whole evening. It was so perfect, I wanted to go back to the beginning of it and do the whole thing over again.

And then, my traitorous brain started having thoughts that weren't so enjoyable. My newly forming relationship with Micah was so special to me that I started having thoughts about things that could take it away. I thought about him going to work at Gina's house next week. I thought about how beautiful she was and knew she was the type who'd take advantage of having him as a captive audience. I imagined that home-cooked meal she and her mother would make. It would probably taste really good, and I was sure they would be super sweet and accommodating to Micah and his crew.

I found myself feeling agitated and nervous until a random thought crossed my mind. It was a simple thought, but it gave me enough peace of mind to stop worrying about it and fall asleep. I thought if God truly wanted me to end up with Micah, then neither Gina nor anyone else would be able to interfere. If we were supposed to end up together, then we would. Period. I certainly wouldn't be able to control every pretty girl who crossed his path. All I could do was be myself, and if we were meant to be, then that would be enough.

I slept like a rock once that thought sunk in, and woke up just before 9am to Roscoe stirring and sniffing at my arm. I glanced at my alarm clock and moaned something to my fuzzy little early bird about letting me get some rest on a Saturday. I stayed there for a few minutes, trying to go back to sleep before deciding it was hopeless.

I picked up my phone from the nightstand and smiled as I stared down at it, noticing I already had a text from Micah. I wiped the sleep from my eyes and blinked, focusing on the screen.

Micah: "Good morning sunshine. Call me when you get up."

I instantly forgot all about how mad I was at Roscoe for waking me up. I reached over to pet his belly and spoke to him as if he was the best dog in the world. "He called me sunshine," I told Roscoe, cooing tone that made it sound like I was talking to him. His tail started thumping against my leg. "And he said I should call him," I added, still using baby talk.

Roscoe was either overjoyed to hear the news or overjoyed by my excitement. He got to his feet and stared down at me with a wagging tail and what looked like a smile on his face.

"I'll take you out in a minute," I said. I pressed the appropriate buttons to call Micah and cleared my throat once or twice, making sure my voice would work.

"There she is," he said, answering his phone.

The sound of his voice sent instant shivers through my body.

"Good morning," I said, my voice betraying how sleepy I was.

"Did you just wake up?" he asked.

"Yeah, and I wasn't happy about it either— Roscoe's in big trouble."

He laughed. "He woke you up?"

"Yeah, he's used to my school schedule, so he stinks at sleeping in."

"Why don't you bring him over for breakfast?" he asked.

I smiled, loving the possibility of seeing him this soon. "At your house?" I asked.

"Why not? I have eggs and bacon, and cereal and all that stuff. You wanna come over?"

"You talked me into it."

"It was the bacon, right?"

I laughed. "Give me a few minutes to get dressed. Text me your address."

"All right. I'll see you in a few," he said.

"Sounds good."

I had a huge smile on my face as I said goodbye and hung up the phone. "You wanna go to Micah's?" I asked Roscoe, petting him and getting him all pumped up just by the tone of my voice. He sprang off the bed and back onto it waiting for me to take him wherever we were going.

We had a small fenced yard and I put Roscoe outside so I could get dressed in peace. I pulled on skinny jeans, Chuck Taylors, and an Adidas hoodie, and put my hair into a quick messy bun high on my head.

I put on a little foundation, mascara, and lip-gloss since that was all I ever wore anyway. I read in a magazine one time that if you only did one thing to your face, you needed to curl your eyelashes. I went out and bought one of those little curler tools that same day, and ever since then, I always did it. It was years ago when I read that, but it was one of those things that stuck with me. I didn't have many beauty rituals, but curling my eyelashes was one of them.

It took me less than 10 minutes to reach Micah's house. I knew his business was relatively new, so I was taken aback by how nice his place was. It looked to be as big as the house I was sharing with three other roommates, and caught myself feeling curious about the concrete business. Micah's truck must have been parked in the garage, because mine was the only car in the driveway. I checked his address again just to make sure I hadn't made a mistake.

Once I got a good view of the front porch, I knew it was Micah's. Under my feet, was the most beautiful stained concrete I'd ever seen. It was a wide porch that ran most of the length of the house. It had a big sweeping swirl pattern that was stained several shades of brown and mahogany. I never realized concrete was an art form, but obviously it was. I stared down at it knowing for sure Micah's hands had created it.

He opened the door, and while still staring at the floor, I said, "This is so beautiful!"

"The porch was my guinea pig," he said. "You should see the basement."

I glanced at him to find that he was stooping to greet Roscoe. He was wearing athletic clothes—a pair of fitted sweatpants and a black, long sleeved Nike t-shirt.

"You look sporty," I said.

We made eye contact for the first time when I said that, and I was surprised again at the sight of his face. It was like every time I was away from him I forgot how handsome he was, and when I saw him again it took me off guard.

"I went to the gym earlier," he said, smiling.

"You already went to the gym?" I asked, unable to comprehend that sort of dedication.

"You look sporty too," he said, pinching my hoodie, as he straightened to stand next to me.

"Yeah, but I didn't earn it," I said. "I just rolled out of bed and put this on."

His eyes roamed over my face as he took me in with that confident, easy smile I loved so much. "You wanna come in?"

I nodded and followed him through the threshold. "I really can't believe how nice this house is," I said. "I should have gotten into concrete instead of teaching."

He glanced at me with a grin. "My business is doing well, but I'm not at this level yet."

My expression was curious, and he continued.

"I got a settlement from the accident."

"Oh, I'm sorry," I said, feeling bad at the turn the conversation had taken.

He smiled, but it didn't quite reach his eyes. "Don't be," he said. "It was a crazy, life-changing experience, but I'm starting to appreciate the bigger picture. Natalie's better off where she is, and my life is what it is because of the path I've taken."

Roscoe ran to check out the rest of the house as Micah and I walked toward the kitchen. "Is he okay?" I asked. Micah nodded. I didn't want to brush by the subject while he was being so open, so I said, "Appreciating the bigger picture is a gift—I'm getting there myself, and there's a lot to be said for it."

I sat on a barstool while Micah made breakfast. Roscoe checked out the house for several minutes but ultimately decided he wanted to be in there with us and curled up on a rug by the sink.

Micah was a clown of the first degree. He made up an impromptu breakfast song while he was cooking. It was so cool and he sang it so well that I asked him where he heard it. He laughed like he thought my question was cute and said he made it up.

The weather was crisp and beautiful, and we spent the entire day together. Micah had some yard work to do and needed to wash his truck, but he said he wanted me to hang out while he did it. I pulled some weeds for him while he got his chores done. He had a fenced yard that was three times the size of mine, and Roscoe thought he'd died and gone to heaven.

It was the first day I spent at Micah's house, but I felt the oddest sense of comfort, like I'd been there a thousand times. No sense of comfort could prepare me for the shock I felt at the first sight of his beautiful basement floors. It was mid afternoon by the time he gave me the official tour of the house, which ended with the basement.

"I didn't even know stain came in this many colors!" I said, staring slack-jawed at the unbelievable floors. An intricate design with swirls and stars had been cut into the concrete, and the colors of stain that accentuated the design were absolutely breathtaking. There was brown, black, blue, red, gold, green and orange—a rainbow of colors.

"You like it?" he asked.

"It's… I'm…" I stammered. "Did you seriously make this with your own hands?"

I looked at him and saw that he was smiling. "You like it?"

"It's really the most beautiful thing I've ever seen. It should be in an art gallery or something. You should have people over every night just so they can appreciate it."

"I have you to appreciate it," he said, drawing me into his arms. I went willingly, hanging onto him as if I never wanted to let go. He'd been working outside, and I breathed in a wonderful mix of his shower gel and deodorant mixed with a distinctly masculine smell from excursion. *What sort of man was he that even his sweat smelled good?* I squeezed him tightly, hoping his scent was rubbing off on my shirt so I could revisit it once I got home.

We ate dinner together before Roscoe and I left. I didn't want to leave, but I had some things to tend to at home, and this fairytale day had to come to an end at some point.

Micah kissed me as I was leaving. It was amazing and knee-buckling, but it wasn't as passionate as the one we shared in my driveway, and

I knew he was trying to hold back for the sake of propriety. My urges wanted to say to heck with propriety, but I knew Micah and I were doing the right thing by taking it slow.

Trish was at home when I got back. Ryan was there too, but he must've been in his room because Trish was the only one in the living room. She had text me earlier, so she knew where I had been.

"Did you stay at his house all day? She asked as soon as I walked in the door grinning from ear to ear.

She called Roscoe over, and he jumped on the couch to greet her. "We got out once to get some tire cleaning stuff at an auto supply store, but other than that we stayed at his house. It's beautiful. You should see it. I'll have to take you over there sometime. It's not far from here."

She loved on Roscoe as she listened to me, so I continued.

"He did some concrete work in his house, and it's the coolest thing I've ever seen. I didn't even know you could do that with concrete."

"When are you gonna see him again?"

"I'm going to church with him in the morning."

She smiled at me and lifted her eyebrows. "I'm technically not going with him because he's singing, and he has to be there really early, but I'm meeting him at the late service. Do you want to come? We're planning on having lunch with his parents afterward, and I know they wouldn't mind if you come."

She shook her head. "Maybe sometime, but I have plans to go on a hike with Shane tomorrow if it doesn't rain."

"What do you think I should wear?" I asked.

She shrugged. "I think you'd be fine in jeans. I don't think you have to wear your Sunday best to church nowadays."

Chapter 20

I'd been excited about going to church, but now that I was in the car on my way there, I was feeling reluctant and fearful, and wondering why I ever agreed to go there in the first place.

I gave some serious consideration to texting Micah and telling him I couldn't make it—especially when I pulled into the parking lot. I'd seen this place from the road before. I knew it was big, but pulling into the parking lot made me experience a whole new wave of doubt. I was in over my head. I didn't even know what door to enter through, much less how to find the Bennetts. I hadn't even thought to ask Micah if his parents would be there. I just assumed they would and it would be easy to find them, but the prospect of that didn't look so good now that I saw the size of this place.

I pulled into a parking spot and sat there for a few seconds, seriously considering leaving before I opened the door and made myself put one foot in front of the other. I saw people entering through a main door, but I imagined them putting some sort of sash over me that proclaimed I was a first time visitor, so went for one of the doors off to the side in hopes of drawing as little attention to myself as possible.

My plan of attack was to get to the side of the main auditorium so I could try to spot the Bennetts.

If I couldn't find them, I'd slip into a spot where I could disappear.

I was walking down a long hallway toward an open set of doors when I saw a ladies room. I decided to take a second to check my face and hair one last time, and while I was at it, I used the restroom. I didn't really have to go, but I was taking my sweet time getting to the service.

My heart sank when I went to the sink to wash my hands after using the restroom. You would know that Gina Young would be standing at the row of sinks staring at herself in the mirror.

A rush of nerves and frustration washed over me, but I kept my expression neutral as if I hadn't even seen her. I turned on the sink, staring down at my hands the whole time.

"I wonder if God likes it when people start coming to church just to check out guys," she said.

I knew the comment was directed toward me, and I could feel hot blood rising to my face. I absolutely couldn't believe I heard her right. I glanced at her through the reflection in the mirror, but she was just staring at herself as if she hadn't spoken at all. My first instinct was to forget about washing my hands and walk out of the restroom without saying a word to her, but it felt like that'd be letting her win, and was just too stubborn for that.

"I wonder if God likes it when Christians try to discourage new people from coming to church," I retorted, praying my voice didn't betray how nervous I was.

She turned to glare at me with an ice-cold expression that I returned as best I could even though that type of thing was way out of my element.

"God probably doesn't mind if I discourage the new people who are here to see Micah Bennett instead of Him," she said.

I wanted to blow my top, but I regarded her calmly with a slight smile that only made her scowl deepen. "You can think what you want to think, but I'm here for church," I said. "I can see Micah any time I want. I don't have to wait for Sunday."

I came really close to adding that I didn't have to hire him to build a patio at my house either, but I kept that to myself.

She huffed, and said, "You wish," as she turned on her heel and headed for the door, leaving me speechless and shaken.

Another lady came in just as she left and I was grateful she hadn't come in sooner. I numbly finished washing my hands, contemplating whether or not I should stay at the service or call it a day. Something felt wrong about going to a church service as angry as I was.

As I had that thought, an older lady came out of one of the stalls. I didn't know how much she had heard, so I tried to get out of there as quickly as possible. I gave her a quick nod of acknowledgement as I pulled a paper towel from the dispenser.

"Are you the young lady who's new here, or the one who's rude?" she asked.

It took me a second to register her question and once I did, I gave her a smile. "It's my first time here," I said.

She gave me an understanding smile. "Let me fill you in on a little secret," she said. "Just because someone goes to church doesn't mean they're a Christian, and just because someone's a Christian doesn't mean they're nice or they act the way you think they should act. Don't put your expectations on any man, because he, or she, will fail you every time." She reached out and patted me on the arm. "God's the only one who won't disappoint."

I offered her a smile. "Thanks," I said.

"You're not thinking about leaving are you?" she asked.

"No ma'am," I said, even though I most assuredly had been.

She smiled. "Good."

The service was just about to start when I found a seat. I wanted to go home, but I told the lady I'd stay, so I did. I glanced around for the Bennetts, but the place was huge, and it was a lost cause. It crossed my mind to look for the nice couple I met at the festival or Ms. Joan, but I didn't see anyone I recognized.

I watched in awe as Micah led the worship. His story about Bach was at the forefront of my mind because he was so gorgeous, talented, and natural up there, but it was obvious that his goal was God's glory and not his own. His humbleness only served to make me love him even more.

Micah sang four songs before the pastor took the stage. He was a tall, lanky man who looked to be in his fifties. He was funny and entertaining, and I caught myself feeling surprised that I was having a good time.

It was about twenty minutes into the message when I felt a hand on my shoulder. "Scoot over and let me sit here," I heard a voice whisper in my ear.

I smiled and shifted over a chair so Micah could sit on the end next to me. Relief flooded my body as soon as he sat down. He reached out and squeezed my thigh right above my knee once he sat down.

"You were impossible to find out here," he whispered. "I thought you'd be with my parents."

"I couldn't find them," I whispered back.

"They always sit on the other side," he said, leaving his hand possessively on my leg. "That's why it took me forever to find you."

I smiled at him. "I'm glad you did."

We focused on the message, and before long it was over. We walked out of the sanctuary holding hands, which made my nerves buzz like they did every single time he touched me.

"Did you like it?" he asked, on our way to the parking lot.

"I loved it," I said smiling.

I didn't plan on telling him or anyone else about the confrontation I had with Gina, since it wasn't even worth it.

He and I had driven separate cars, so we decided he would follow me to my house where I would drop off my car and ride with him to eat with his parents. Micah asked me why I wasn't bringing Roscoe along when I climbed into his truck, and I told him the spoiled mutt had gone on a hike with Trish and her boyfriend and would probably eat steak for lunch.

I was anxious as we pulled up in his parents' driveway. I didn't know how much he had told them about us seeing each other, if anything, and I couldn't help but wonder how they would feel about it. I caught myself doubting whether or not we could actually be classified as 'seeing each other', and figured I'd try to keep quiet and let him do most of the talking.

Micah waited for me to come around the front of the truck and he took my hand to lead me to his parents' front door.

Every light in the house was on, and the TV was tuned to what looked like a pregame show for a football game. His dad was standing in front of the screen with a remote in his hand, and he turned to face us when we came in the door. His eye instantly snapped to the place where Micah's hand held mine.

I felt suddenly insecure, and as if Micah sensed it, his grip tightened. Mr. Jesse smiled and cocked his chin up to yell in the direction of the kitchen.

"Micah and Carly are here!" he yelled. We dropped hands and began to take our shoes off.

"Micahhh! Carlyyy!" I heard Thomas announce walking from the kitchen to the living room to greet us.

I knew even before I saw him that his hands would be lifted high above his head, and they most certainly were. A huge smile spread across my face as I crossed the living room to meet him and give him a hug.

"We're gonna have lunch," he said. "Can you come eat with us?"

I nodded. "I think so, if that's okay with you."

"Yes it is. Are we doing science class too?" Before I had the chance to answer, his attention shifted to Micah. "How did you get here at the same time as my baby brother?"

"We rode together," Micah said, coming to stand beside me.

Thomas stared at him as if it didn't quite register. "My baby brother sang songs at church today," he said, obviously having other things on his mind.

"I know," I said. "I saw him."

His eyes widened and his jaw dropped. "You saw him?"

"Yeah," I said. "I went to your church this morning."

"To my church?" Thomas asked, still shocked.

Claire came in the living room with her apron on to give out hugs. "Hey guys!" she said smiling and thankfully not acting surprised to see us together. She gave us hugs one by one and told Micah what a "beautiful job" he did that morning.

"Carly went to our church," Thomas said, talking to his mom.

"I know she did," Claire said smiling. "She came with Micah."

Thomas looked at me with wide, speculative eyes. "You came to my church with my baby brother?"

I smiled and nodded. "Are you okay with that?" I asked, tentatively.

Micah put his arm around my shoulders and gave me a squeeze. "Carly and I are gonna be together a lot from now on, brother."

I could see Thomas' wheels turning as he took us in with a serious expression. He stood there for several long seconds before he said, "Are you and Carly gonna get married?"

Micah looked at me with a smile, and I regarded him with shock, wondering how he'd possibly respond to his brother's question. "I haven't asked her yet," he said, not taking his eyes from mine, "but I'm sure we will. Don't you think?"

My heart was beating faster than ever before as adrenaline and sheer joy pumped through my body in waves. I smiled, hoping I was holding up. I was looking at Micah, but I knew Claire, Jesse, and Thomas were all staring at us, waiting for my answer.

"I think that's a definite possibility," I said, trying my hardest not to cry or say the wrong thing.

Micah smiled and squeezed me again as he turned his attention to his brother. "We will," he assured his family, nodding confidently.

Claire let out a happy screech and put her hands over her mouth before reaching out to hug us again. "That's so sweet," she said.

I glanced at Thomas, who was still staring at us, contemplating everything with an earnest expression. I had no idea what he was thinking.

"If you get married," he said, "what will she be?"

"That'll make her my wife," Micah said.

Thomas regarded us with a look of confusion and frustration as if Micah hadn't answered the question.

"Will she be my family?"

"Oh, you mean what will she be *to you*?" Micah said, understanding. "When we get married, she'll be your sister."

Thomas stood still for a second and then pointed at me. "Carly will be my sister?" he asked.

"Yeah," Micah said. "How's that sound?"

And just like that, Thomas scrunched up his face and lifted his fist to hold his wrinkled up nose. He let out a long, high-pitched wheezing cry that I easily recognized as the signal that he was overwhelmed

217

with happiness. He took in a breath of air through his mouth and let out another cry, keeping his face buried in his hand.

I was helpless to stop the tears from flowing out of my own eyes. The sight of him so overjoyed at having me as his sister touched my heart so deeply that I cried right along with him.

I hugged him tightly, and he squeezed me back, alternating between wheezing a cry and breathing in. I pulled back and put a kiss on his cheek, doing my best to compose myself as I took in this precious soul.

"When are you getting married?" he asked, wiping at his face with his shirtsleeve. "Tomorrow?"

"We haven't really talked about that yet—" I started to say.

But Micah cut me off. "Soon," he said.

"Tomorrow?" Thomas asked again, looking at Micah who smiled.

"Not tomorrow, but soon."

"This is so exciting, but my green beans are burning," Claire said wringing her hands as she reluctantly turned to head for the kitchen. "You guys come in here!" she called from over her shoulder.

Thomas immediately obeyed his mom's request and walked off in the direction she'd gone, still wiping at his face.

Micah grabbed my hands and pulled me to him, looking down at me, smiling. "I'll probably catch some football with my dad," he said. "You can go see what my mom's up to or stay in here with me."

I smiled and glanced toward the kitchen and then to his dad, who was preoccupied with the television again. "I'll probably go see if your mom needs any help," I said.

He squeezed my hand as he bent to put a quick kiss on my lips. His mouth was soft and warm, and I couldn't imagine myself being any happier than I was at that very moment.

"I love you," he whispered, smiling down at me.

Okay, so I take that back. This moment just officially got happier.

I popped up to give him one more kiss on the cheek. "I love you too," I whispered back.

Epilogue

Three weeks later.

It was 2:00 in the afternoon, and I was teaching 28 eleventh grade students. They were my most difficult group this year, but earning their respect proved a rewarding venture. They were a rowdy bunch, so I had to be on top of my game everyday to keep their attention. It was the day before we got out of school for our Thanksgiving break, so they were especially amped. They were my last class of the day, and I told them we'd have some free time at the end of class if they let me get through my lecture and seemed like they were paying attention.

I was talking about the relation of temperature and pressure when I heard a knock on my classroom door.

"Everybody stay quiet," I warned as I crossed to open it. I figured it was someone wanting to borrow something. I had a little window so I could see into the hallway, but a picture of a turkey holding a bubbling beaker that one of my students painted in art class currently blocked it.

I opened the door, feeling slightly frustrated that I had been interrupted during my lecture and would now have to work to get their attention again. I found Micah standing on the other side smiling at me. A smile spread across my face as I glanced back into the classroom to make sure everything was still under control. I looked back at Micah with wide eyes.

"What are you doing here?" I whispered.

"I came to see you. Can I come in?"

I glanced at the students again, who were now looking at me curiously. They couldn't see who I was talking to, and a few of them were leaning over their desks and craning their necks as they tried to get a glimpse.

Micah took a giant step past me and peered around me to see the students. I watched in surprise as he smiled at them. "Do you guys mind if I come in for a second?" he asked.

Most of the class yelled, "No," at the same time, but a few of the girls let out whistles and calls of approval that made me smile and roll my eyes.

Micah was standing right next to me, and he looked at me with a huge smile. "I'm sorry to interrupt your class," he said, not seeming regretful at all. "I'll just be a minute." He put a hand around my back and pulled me close to give me a quick kiss on the check, which drew whoops and whistles of approval.

"Just sit right there," he said, gesturing to my desk. "I have to grab something from the hallway."

He walked out the door, and one of the girls yelled out, "Is that your boyfriend?"

Another one yelled, "He's hot!" a statement that was followed by murmuring, clapping, and laughing.

"Shhhh!" I said, turning to them with wide eyes but an underlying smile.

Everyone was quiet as we watched Micah enter the room carrying an acoustic guitar. They let out another round of catcalls as he walked to my desk. He propped himself on the corner of it and patted the spot next to him, telling me to sit.

I smiled and obeyed, but nerves and adrenaline were already taking over my body. I could only think of one reason why he'd bring a guitar into my classroom, but I didn't want to get my hopes up.

"I have a Thanksgiving song to share with you guys if you don't mind," Micah said.

And there went that idea.

I continued to smile. The students made various noises and whistled as he positioned his guitar under his arm and gave it a strum.

He began to sing and play, which shut them up completely. They were thoroughly entranced from the first note. He was hilarious as usual and had them laughing with lyrics that had to do with turkeys and Pilgrims and the poor Indians who got the short end of the stick.

Then he shifted to look at me and, in song, admitted that he wasn't there to sing about Thanksgiving at all. He said he was there to sing a love song and went into lyrics that were equally as funny, but all focused on how awesome I was and how much he loved me. I laughed to keep from crying as I glanced back-and-forth between him and my students, trying to take it in.

Several of them had taken out their phones and we're recording the whole thing. It was all such a blur of wonderful excitement that I had trouble taking in all of the lyrics. All I know is that it ended with, "And hopefully pretty soon you'll be calling her Mrs. Bennett."

Before I knew what was happening, he set his guitar on the desk behind him and reached in his pocket for a ring box before getting down on one knee.

The students erupted in a chorus of cheers. Unable to believe what was happening, I put my hands over my eyes, peeking through my fingers.

"Carly Howard, I love you something terrible," he said. "Will you please, please be my—"

I cut him off before he could say it. "Yes!" I said, pulling him to his feet.

He stood and gathered me into his arms.

My students were going insane. I could hear them yelling things out.

"That was off the chain!"

"Dude, he just proposed!"

"Ms. Howard's getting hitched, y'all!"

"I videoed almost that whole song!"

"Send me that. I'm gonna use that song to propose to my old lady!"

I tried to hold back the tears as I pulled back to stare up at him. I couldn't believe he was once untouchable, and now he was mine.

He smiled at me and leaned in for a kiss. My first instinct was to break the kiss right away since I wasn't sure how appropriate it was in front of my students, but once his were lips on mine, I just couldn't bring myself to pull back. My knees grew weak, and I was unable to do anything but relish the feel of his perfect, warm lips on mine.

Another round of yells went up, but neither Micah nor I paid attention to it. He put his hands on my face and kissed me tenderly as if he couldn't bear to let me go.

The cheering grew louder and finally, we managed to pull our lips apart. We smiled at each other for a second before I looked at the classroom full of ecstatic students.

One of the girls, who happened to be the most beautiful, popular girl in school, was using her notebook to fan her face with one hand and had her other hand raised high.

"Yes, Emma?" I asked.

"Does he have a twin brother?" she asked, pointing at Micah.

Everyone cracked up.

I smiled. "There's only one of him," I said trying my best to look regretful.

Emma, along with the other girls in the class had no shame whatsoever making a few last love-struck comments as Micah said goodbye and went for the door.

He thanked them on his way out for letting him interrupt class and wished them all a happy Thanksgiving.

The final bell would be ringing before too long, and I knew there was no sense in trying to finish my lecture, so I told them we'd get to it after the break. We spent the rest of the class with me answering personal questions, most of which were about Micah. The girls were interested in seeing my ring, so I let them pass it around the classroom so they could take a look.

A few of the students had managed to get most of his song on the video, and we watched it together. I told those who captured it to email it to me so I could watch it anytime I wanted, and they all promised they would. They couldn't believe how good it was and went on and on about how he should be a famous singer.

The final bell rang, and after taking a couple of minutes to pack up my things, I was on my way to the parking lot. I was wearing a smile as I thought about his song and how it was written just for me.

Then suddenly I noticed that Micah was standing in the parking lot. He was leaning casually on the front fender of my car, and smiling as he watched me approach.

"You are unbelievable," I said, when I was close enough for him to hear me.

He looked like a dream sitting there leaning against my car, and I just couldn't believe he was mine—officially mine with a ring and everything.

"You're unbelievable," he returned. "I loved seeing you in there. Your students love you."

"They love you too," I said, walking straight into his open arms. "Where's your car?" I asked looking up at him.

"I had Blake drop me off after work so I could ride home with you."

"What if I would have said no?" I asked.

He gave me a sly grin. "You wouldn't have."

"You know that?" I asked.

"Yep."

"Why, because I'm crazy about you?"

He shrugged. "Because you're supposed to belong to me."

"And now it's official?" I asked, holding my hand in the air to examine my new ring.

"I wouldn't call it official just yet."

"We still have to get married, huh?"

"Yep."

"When's that gonna happen?" I asked.

"Whenever you want," he said squeezing me.

"Let's do it soon," I said. "Maybe by next Christmas."

"Next Christmas?" he asked, looking down at me as if I were crazy. "Like a year from now? That's not soon."

"I thought that was soon," I said. "I assumed it took a while to plan a wedding, and thought people might think we were rushing into it if we did it any sooner."

"Since when do you care what people think?" he asked.

I shrugged and smiled shyly. "Do you want to do it sooner?" I asked.

He laughed. "I'm ready to do it yesterday," he said.

"Me too," I said, "I just didn't want anyone to think—"

"I don't care what they think," he said. "And nobody's gonna think anything anyway."

"What about Christmas then. Or maybe New Years?"

"Like in a few weeks?" he asked.

I shrugged. "Or whatever you were thinking," I said.

"Christmas sounds great. The sooner the better as far as I'm concerned."

I smiled at him and bit my lip. "I can't believe we're doing it."

"I can," he said. "It's the most natural thing in the world to me."

I stared up at him. "I'm gonna be a good wife to you," I said.

"I know you will," he said, smiling.

He placed a gentle kiss on my lips. It was an unspoken promise that he'd be good to me too.

Everything had happened really quickly between us, but it was flawless—a seamless plan by The Master Planner. Maybe it took some tears to get us there, but they now seemed like a distant memory. I was right where I was supposed to be, and so was he.

The End
(till book 2)

S.D.G.

A big thanks to my awesome team. Chris, Jan, and Glenda... you're the best!

Made in the USA
Lexington, KY
13 May 2017